ACCLAIM FOR GAIL BOWEN AND
THE JOANNE KILBOURN MYSTERIES

"Bowen is one of those rare, magical mystery writers readers love not only for her suspense skills but for her stories' elegance, sense of place and true-to-life form. . . . A master of ramping up suspense" — *Ottawa Citizen*

"Bowen can confidently place her series beside any other being produced in North America." — Halifax *Chronicle-Herald*

"Gail Bowen's Joanne Kilbourn mysteries are small works of elegance that assume the reader of suspense is after more than blood and guts, that she is looking for the meaning behind a life lived and a life taken." *Calgary Herald*

"Bowen has a hard eye for the way human ambition can take advantage of human gullibility." — *Publishers Weekly*

"Gail Bowen got the recipe right with her series on Joanne Kilbourn." — *Vancouver Sun*

"What works so well [is Bowen's] sense of place – Regina comes to life – and her ability to inhabit the everyday life of an interesting family with wit and vigour. . . . Gail Bowen continues to be a fine mystery writer, with a protagonist readers can invest in for the long run." — *National Post*

"Gail Bowen is one of Canada's literary treasures." — *Ottawa Citizen*

OTHER JOANNE KILBOURN MYSTERIES
BY GAIL BOWEN

# MURDER AT THE MENDEL

## A Joanne Kilbourn Mystery

# GAIL BOWEN

McClelland & Stewart

Copyright © 1991 by Gail Bowen
First published by Douglas & McIntyre Ltd., 1991

First M&S paperback edition published 1992
This edition published 2011

**Library and Archives Canada Cataloguing in Publication**

Bowen, Gail, 1942-
Murder at the Mendel : a Joanne Kilbourn mystery / Gail Bowen.

ISBN 978-0-7710-1321-8

I. Title.

PS8553.08995M87 2011    C813'.54    C2011-900300-7

We acknowledge the financial support of the Government of Canada
through the Book Publishing Industry Development Program and that
of the Government of Ontario through the Ontario Media Development
Corporation's Ontario Book Initiative. We further acknowledge the
support of the Canada Council for the Arts and the Ontario Arts
Council for our publishing program.

Published simultaneously in the United States of America by
McClelland & Stewart Ltd., P.O. Box 1030, Plattsburgh, New York 12901

Library of Congress Control Number: 2011925594

This book was produced using ancient-forest friendly paper.
Typeset in Trump Mediaeval by M&S, Toronto
Printed and bound in Canada

McClelland & Stewart Ltd.
75 Sherbourne Street
Toronto, Ontario
M5A 2P9
www.mcclelland.com

1 2 3 4 5    15 14 13 12 11

*For my grandmother, Hilda Bartholomew,*
*and*
*my friends Maggie Siggins and Joanne Bonneville,*
*thanks*

# MURDER AT THE MENDEL

# CHAPTER

# 1

If I hadn't gone back to change my shoes, it would have been me instead of Izaak Levin who found them dying. But halfway to the Loves' cottage I started worrying that shoes with heels would make me too tall to dance with, and by the time I got back to the Loves', Izaak was standing in their doorway with the dazed look of a man on the edge of shock. When I pushed past him into the cottage, I saw why.

I was fifteen years old, and I had never seen a dead man, but I knew Desmond Love was dead. He was sitting in his place at the dining-room table, but his head lolled back on his neck as if something critical had come loose, and his mouth hung open as if he were sleeping or screaming. His wife, Nina, was in the chair across from him. She was always full of grace, and she had fallen so that her head rested against the curve of her arm as it lay on the table. She was beautiful, but her skin was waxen, and I could hear the rattle of her breathing in that quiet room. My friend Sally was lying on the floor. She had vomited; she was pale and her breathing was laboured, but I knew she wouldn't die. She was thirteen years old, and you don't die when you're thirteen.

It was Nina I went to. My relationship with my own mother had never been easy, and Nina had been my refuge for as long as I could remember. I took her in my arms and began to cry and call her name. Izaak Levin was still standing in the doorway, but seeing me with Nina seemed to jolt him back to reality.

"Joanne, you have to get your father. We need a doctor here," he said.

My legs felt heavy, the way they do in a dream when you try to run and you can't, but somehow I got to our cottage and brought my father. He was a methodical and reassuring man, and as I watched him taking pulses, looking into pupils, checking breathing, I felt better.

"What happened?" he asked Izaak Levin.

Izaak shook his head. When he spoke, his voice was dead with disbelief. "I don't know. I took the boat over to town for a drink before dinner. When I got back, I found them like this." He pointed to a half-filled martini pitcher on the table. At Sally's place there was a glass with an inch of soft drink in the bottom. "He must have put it in the drinks. I guess he decided it wasn't worth going on, and he wanted to take them with him."

There was no need to explain the pronouns. My father and I knew what he meant. At the beginning of the summer Desmond Love had suffered a stroke that had slurred his speech, paralyzed his right side and, most seriously, stilled his hand. He was forty years old, a bold and innovative maker of art and a handsome and immensely physical man. It was believable that, in his rage at the ravages of the stroke, he would kill himself, and so I stored away Izaak's explanation. I stored it away in the same place I stored the other memories of that night: the animal sound of retching Nina made after my father forced the ipecac into her mouth. The silence broken only by a loon's cry as my father and Izaak carried the Loves, one by one, down to the motorboat at the dock. The blaze of the sunset on the lake as my father wrapped Nina and Sally in the blankets they kept in the boat for picnics. The terrible emptiness in Desmond Love's eyes as they looked at the September sky.

And then my father, standing in the boat, looking at me on the dock, "Joanne, you're old enough to know the truth here: Sally will be all right, but Des is dead and I'm not sure about Nina's chances. It'll be better for you later if you don't ride in this boat tonight." His voice was steady, but there were tears in his eyes. Desmond Love had been his best friend since they were boys. "I want you to go back home and wait for me. Just tell your mother there's been an emergency. Don't tell her . . ."

"The truth." I finished the sentence for him. The truth would make my mother start drinking. So would a lie. It never took much.

"Don't let Nina die," I said in an odd, strangled voice.

"I'll do all I can," he said, and then the quiet of the night was shattered by the roar of the outboard motor; the air was filled with the smell of gasoline, and the boat, low in the water from its terrible cargo, began to move across the lake into the brilliant gold of the sunset. It was the summer of 1958, and I was alone on the dock, waiting.

* * *

Thirty-two years later I was walking across the bridge that links the university community to the city of Saskatoon. It was the night of the winter solstice. The sky was high and starless, and there was a bone-chilling wind blowing down the South Saskatchewan River from the north. I was on my way to the opening of an exhibition of the work of Sally Love.

As soon as I turned onto Spadina Crescent, I could see the

bright letters of her name on the silk banners suspended over the entrance to the Mendel Gallery: Sally Love. Sally Love. Sally Love. There was something festive and celebratory about those paint-box colours, but as I got closer I saw there were other signs, too, and some of them weren't so pretty. These signs were mounted on stakes held by people whose faces shone with zeal, and their crude lettering seemed to pulse with indignation: "Filth Belongs in Toilets Not on Walls," "Jail Pornographers," "No Room for Love Here" and one that said simply, "Bitch."

A crowd had gathered. Some people were attempting a counterattack, and every so often a voice, thin and self-conscious in the winter air, would raise itself in a tentative defence: "What about freedom of the arts?" "We're not a police state yet!" "The only real obscenity is censorship."

A TV crew had set up under the lights of the entrance and they were interviewing a soft-looking man in a green tuque with the Hilltops logo and a nylon ski jacket that said "Silver Broom: Saskatoon '90." The man was one of our city councillors, and as I walked up I could hear his spiritless baritone spinning out the clichés for the ten o'clock news: "Community standards . . . public property . . . our children's innocence . . . privacy of the home . . ." The councillor's name was Hank Mewhort, and years before I had been at a political fundraiser where he had dressed as a leprechaun to deliver the financial appeal. As I walked carefully around the camera crew, Hank's sanctimonious bleat followed me. I had liked him better as a leprechaun.

When I handed my invitation to a commissionaire posted at the entrance, he checked my name off on a list and opened the gallery door for me. As I started through, I felt a sharp blow in the middle of my back. I turned and found myself facing a fresh-faced woman with a sweet and vacant smile. She was grasping her sign so the shaft was in front of her like a broadsword. She came at me again, but then, very quickly, a city cop grabbed her from behind and led her off into the night. She was still smiling. Her sign lay on the concrete in front of me, its message carefully spelled out in indelible marker the colour of dried blood: "The Wages of Sin is Death." I shuddered and pulled my coat tight around me.

Inside, all was light and airiness and civility. People dressed in holiday evening clothes greeted one another in the reverent tones Canadians use at cultural events. A Douglas fir, its boughs luminous with yellow silk bows, filled the air with the smell of Christmas. In front of the tree was an easel with a handsome poster announcing the Sally Love exhibition. Propped discreetly against it was a small placard stating that Erotobiography was in Gallery III at the rear of the building and that patrons must be eighteen years of age to be admitted.

Very prim. Very innocent. But this small addendum to Sally's show had eclipsed everything else. To the left of the Douglas fir, a wall plastered with newspaper clippings told the story: Erotobiography consisted of seven pictures Sally Love had painted to record her sexual experiences.

All the pictures were explicit, but the one that had caused the furor was a fresco. A fresco, the local paper noted sternly, is permanent. The colour in a fresco does not rest on the surface; it sinks into and becomes part of the wall. And what Sally Love had chosen to sink into the wall of the publicly owned Mendel Gallery was a painting of the sexual parts of all the people with whom she had been intimate. Erotobiography. According to the newspaper, there were one hundred individual entries, and a handful of the genitalia were female. Nonetheless, community standards being what they are, the work was known by everyone as the Penis Painting.

The exhibition that was opening that night was a large one. Several of the pictures on loan from major galleries throughout North America had been heralded as altering the direction of contemporary art; many of the paintings had been praised for their psychological insights or their technical virtuosity. None of that seemed to matter much. It was the penises that had prompted the people outside to leave their warm living rooms and clutch the shafts of picket signs in their mittened hands. It was the penises the handsome men and women exchanging soft words in the foyer had come to see. As I walked toward the wing where Nina Love and I had agreed to meet, I was smiling. I had to admit that I wanted to see the penises, too. The rest was just foreplay.

The south wing of the Mendel Gallery is a conservatory, a place where you can find green and flowering things even when the temperature sticks at forty below for weeks on end. When I stepped through the door, the moisture and the warmth and the fragrance enveloped me, and for a moment I stood there and let the cold and the tension flow out of my body. Nina Love was sitting on a bench in front of a blazing display of amaryllis, azalea and bird of paradise. She had a compact cupped in her hand, and her attention was wholly focused on her reflection. It was, I thought sadly, becoming her characteristic gesture.

That night as I was getting ready for Sally's opening, I'd heard the actress Diane Keaton answer a radio interviewer's question about how she faced aging. "You have to be very brave," she'd said, and I'd thought of Nina. Much as I cared for her I had to admit that Nina Love wasn't being very brave about growing older.

Until Thanksgiving, when she had come to Saskatoon to help care for her granddaughter, Nina and I had kept in touch mostly through letters and phone calls. I'd seen her only on those rare occasions when I was in Toronto to check on my mother.

Illusions were easy at a distance. I was discovering that up close they were harder to sustain. Nina had aged physically, of course, although I suspected the process had been smoothed somewhat by a surgeon's skill. There were feathery lines in the skin around her dark eyes, a slight sag in the soft skin beneath her jawline. But that seemed to me as inconsequential as it was inevitable. She was still an extraordinarily beautiful woman.

The problem wasn't with Nina's beauty; it was with how much of herself she seemed to have invested in her beauty. I couldn't be with her long without noticing how often her hand smoothed the skin of her neck or how, when she passed a store window, she would seek out her reflection with anxious eyes.

That night at the Mendel as I watched her bending closer to the mirror in her cupped hand, I felt a pang. But Nina had spent a lot of years assuring me that I had value. Now it was my turn. I walked over and sat down beside her.

"You're perfect," I said, and she was. From the smooth line of her dark hair to her dress – high-necked, long-sleeved, meticulously cut from some material that shimmered green and purple and gold in the half light – to her silky stockings and shining kid pumps, Nina Love was as flawless as money and sustained effort could make a woman.

She snapped the compact shut and laughed. "Jo, I can always count on you. You've always been my biggest fan. That's why I was so worried when you were late." Then her face grew serious. "Wasn't that terrifying out there?"

Our knees were almost touching, but I still had to lean toward Nina to hear her. Sally always said that her mother's soft, breathy voice was a trick to get everyone to pay attention to nothing but her. Trick or not, as I listened to Nina that winter evening, I felt the sense of homecoming I always felt when I walked through a door and found her waiting.

At that moment, she was looking at me critically. "You seem to be a little the worse for wear."

"Well, I walked over, and as my grandfather used to say, it's colder than a witch's teat out there. Then I had an encounter with someone exercising her democratic right to jab me in the back with her picket sign."

"Those creatures out there aren't human," she said. "It's been a nightmare for us. Stuart's phone rings at all hours of the day and night. I'm afraid to take the mail out of the mailbox. Even Taylor is being hurt. Yesterday, a little boy at play school told Taylor her mother should be tied up and thrown in the river."

"Oh, no, what did Taylor do?"

"She told the boy that at least *her* mother didn't have a mustache."

I could feel the corners of my mouth begin to twitch. "A mustache?"

"According to Taylor, the boy's mother needs a shave," Nina said dryly. "But, Jo, I'm afraid I'm beyond laughing at any of this. I really wonder what can be going through Sally's mind. First she leaves her husband and child, then she makes a piece of art that outrages everyone and puts Stuart in a terrible position professionally."

"Nina, I don't think you're being fair, at least not about the painting. I don't know much about these things, but from what I read Sally's a hot ticket in the art world now. That fresco must be worth a king's ransom."

"Oh, you're right about that, and of course that's what makes Stuart's position so difficult. He's the director, and the director's duty is to acquire the best. But he also has a board to deal with and a community to appease. Sally could have painted anything else and people would have been all over the place being grateful to her and to Stuart. As they should be. She's an incredible artist. But she has to have her joke. And so she gives the Mendel a gift that could destroy it. Jo, that fresco of Sally's is a real Trojan horse." Nina reached behind her and pulled a faded bloom from an azalea. "I guess I don't have much sense of proportion about this. It's been so terrible for Stuart and, of course, for Taylor."

"But at least they have you, dear," I said. "I'm sure Stuart would have broken into a million pieces if you hadn't been there to make a home for Taylor and for him. You didn't see him in those first weeks after Sally left. He was like a ghost walker. She was the centre of his life . . ."

Nina's face was impassive. "She's always the centre of everybody's life, isn't she? Right from the beginning . . ."

But she didn't finish the sentence. Stuart Lachlan had come into the conservatory.

"Look, there he is at the door. Doesn't he look fine?" she said.

Stu did, indeed, look fine. As I'd told Nina, his suffering after Sally left had been so intense it seemed to mark him physically. But tonight he looked better – tentative, like a man coming back from a long illness, but immaculate again, as he was in the days when he and Sally were together.

He was a handsome man in his late forties, dark-eyed, dark-haired, with the taut body of a swimmer who never misses a day doing laps. He was wearing a dinner jacket and a surprising and beautiful tie and cummerbund of flowered silk. When he leaned over to kiss me, his cheek was smooth, and he smelled of expensive aftershave.

"Merry Christmas, Jo. With everything else that's been going on, the birthday of the Prince of Peace seems to have been lost in the shuffle. But it's good to be able to wish you joy in person. Your coming here to teach was the second best thing to happen this year."

"I don't have to ask you what the first was. Nina's obviously taking wonderful care of you. You look great, Stu, truly."

"Well, the tie and the cummerbund are Nina's gift. Cosmopolitan and unorthodox, like me, she says." He laughed, but he looked at me eagerly, waiting for his compliment.

I smiled past him at Nina, the shameless flatterer. "She's right, as usual. Do you have time to sit with us for a minute?"

"No, I'm afraid it's time for me to make my little talk and get this opening underway. I just came in to get Nina." Then, flawlessly mannered as always, he offered an arm to each of us. "And of course to escort you, Jo."

It had been a long time since I'd needed an escort, but when we walked into the foyer, I was glad Stuart was there for Nina. The picketers had come through the door. They couldn't have been there long because nothing was happening. They had the punchy look of game show contestants who've won the big prize but aren't sure how to get offstage. The people in evening dress were eying them warily, but everything was calm. Then the TV cameras came inside, and the temperature rose. Someone pushed someone else, and little brush fires of violence seemed to break out all over the room. A woman in an exquisite lace evening gown grabbed a picket sign from a young man and threw it to the floor and stomped on it. The young man bent to pull the sign out from under her and knocked her off balance. When she fell, a man who seemed to be her husband took a swing at the young picketer. Then another man swung at the husband and connected. I heard the unmistakable dull crunch of fist hitting bone, and the husband was down. Then the police were all around and it was over.

The lady in lace and her husband were escorted to a police car; the protesters were shepherded outside, and the TV crews started to pack up. Stuart stood beside me, frozen, like a man in shock. Nina tightened her grip on his arm and said in her soft, compelling voice, "Stuart, it's up to you to put things right here; you can still set the tone for the evening.

Now go talk to those TV people before they go. Put things in perspective for them. Then give one of those witty talks you give, and show the board you're in charge."

It was as if someone had flicked a switch in him. He squared his shoulders, straightened his beautiful tie and headed for the cameras.

Nina and I stood together and watched. The show was worth watching. Stu moved into the bright lights at the front of the foyer with the élan of a model in an ad for expensive Scotch, and the speech he made was impressive, full of references to the civilizing power of art, a gallery's need always to go for the best whenever the best presents itself, a director's obligation to exercise his professional judgement and the community's obligation to support that judgement.

Stuart's face was flushed with the joy that comes when you know that, at a significant moment in your life, you're putting the words together right, that what you're feeling and what you're saying are one and the same. And the icing on the cake was that there were cameras grinding away, recording everything for posterity – or at least for the ten o'clock news.

And then, in just the way that the hour of enchantment ends in fairy tales, the heavy glass doors of the gallery opened and Sally Love walked in. One of the news people spotted her and called out, "Sally's here." And that was that. The crowd turned; the cameras swung around to capture her image, and as quickly as they had begun, Stuart's fifteen minutes of fame were over.

There was always an element of the theatrical about Sally. Part of it, of course, was just that she was so physically striking. She was her father's daughter in every way. She had Desmond Love's talent for making art, and she had his looks – the blond hair that seemed to radiate a wild electric energy of its own, the eyes blue as a larkspur flower, the wide and generous mouth, the long-boned animal grace. And like Des, Sally was always the focal point of whatever room she found herself in. The picture always rearranged itself so that Sally was in the foreground, and that night all of us in the gallery foyer found ourselves suddenly peripheral, background figures in yet another portrait of Sally.

She walked straight to where Stuart was standing with the microphone. She had just come back from New Mexico, and she was wearing a Navajo blanket coat that glowed with the colours of the desert: purple, turquoise, orange, blue. She slipped it off and handed it to Stu. He took it wordlessly. Suddenly he was redundant, no longer the champion of freedom of the arts, just a man holding his wife's coat, waiting for his instructions.

Sally was wearing an outfit a Navajo woman might have worn to dance in: soft boots of pale leather, an ankle-length red cotton skirt belted with silver and turquoise and a black velvet shirt open at the neck to show more silver and turquoise at her throat. Her heavy blond hair was parted in the centre and tied, just above each ear, in a butterfly-shaped knot, and she touched one of the butterflies as she leaned forward to kiss her husband's cheek.

"The traditional hairstyle of unmarried women," she said huskily into the microphone. "With all the hassles this exhibit is causing Stu, I thought I'd better start looking for a new man." Then she grinned wickedly. "Number one hundred and one."

There was a burst of nervous laughter. Sally leaned closer to the microphone. "You know, the people outside are having a great time: they're singing hymns and throwing snowballs. Lots of fun. A couple of people even threw snowballs at me. I think they wanted me to stay out there with them. But I wanted to be in here with you. This is our night. We always say that one of the purposes of art is celebration.

Well, let's celebrate." She turned and looked into her husband's face. "Stu?"

Despite himself, Stuart Lachlan smiled, and Sally seized the moment. She slid her arm through her husband's and said, "The director and I are going to find a drink. Why don't you guys join us?" And she led him smoothly out of the foyer toward the exhibition.

Beside me, Nina smoothed the shimmering line of her dress. There was a flicker of anger in her face, but when she spoke, her words were mild.

"Quite a performance," she said.

I had to agree. In the forty-five years since I'd tiptoed into Nina Love's room to look at her new baby daughter, I'd seen many of Sally Love's performances, but even by Sally's standards, this had been a star turn.

# CHAPTER

# 2

It was a lovely party. This was a major show and the gallery had pulled out all the stops. As we walked among the paintings, two men from the caterers circulated carrying silver trays of tiny tourtieres, so hot the juices were bubbling through the top crust, and fluted paper cups holding crabmeat quiches shaped into perfect hearts. In the middle of the main gallery there was a serving table with a round of Cheddar as big as a wagon wheel and platters piled high with grapes and melon slices and strawberries. And there was a bar.

I was watching the bartender grate nutmeg on top of a bowl of eggnog when I heard a familiar voice.

"I know you like strong drink, Joanne. I'll ask Tony to make a Christmas Comfort for you. It's a drink that's out of fashion now but you'll like it."

I turned and found myself face to face with Hilda McCourt, a woman I had met the year before when a man who was dear to both of us had died violently. In the time since, our friendship had become one of the pleasures of my life. She was more than eighty years old and she looked every minute of it, but she always looked great. She was as slender as a high-school girl, and that night she was wearing an outfit a high-school girl would wear: a kind of combat suit made out of some shiny green fabric, very fashionable, and her hair dyed brilliant red was tied back with a swatch of the same material.

"Well, Joanne?" she asked.

"I trust you implicitly," I said, smiling.

"A Christmas Comfort for Mrs. Kilbourn, please, Tony, and another for me. He's an old student," she said as Tony went off to get the ingredients. He warmed a brandy snifter over a fondue pot he had bubbling on his worktable, filled the glass three-quarters full of Southern Comfort, added a slice of lemon and a little boiling water and then warmed the glass again.

"Drink it quickly now, while it's hot," said Hilda.

"There must be three ounces of liquor in that thing. I'll be under the table."

"Don't be foolish," Hilda said impatiently. "Just keep moving and eating." When she shook her head, I noticed that she had tiny golden Christmas tree balls hanging from her earlobes. She took my arm and led me toward the pictures.

"Now, what do you think of all this brouhaha about the fresco?" she asked.

"I haven't seen it yet, but I'm sure it's extraordinary. Everything Sally does is extraordinary."

"I hear ambivalence in your voice."

"Sorry," I said. "I guess when you've had the kind of history Sally and I've had, it takes a while to get rid of the ambivalence."

Hilda raised her eyebrows. "A tale for another time?" she asked.

I smiled. "For another time. Hey, speaking of tales, the one that's unfolding here tonight's pretty engrossing. Those people outside aren't going to be satisfied until someone comes here with a brush and paints over Erotobiography. I wonder what the board's going to do?"

"I can answer that," said Hilda. "The board is going to give Sally a splendid dinner to thank her for her generosity and they're going to issue a statement of support for Stuart Lachlan and then they're going to renew his contract for another five years."

"You sound very certain."

"I am very certain. I'm on the board. I've known most of the other members for years. They're decent people and they're reasonable. A lot of them are from the business community. They may not know a Picasso from a Pollock but they do understand art as investment. That fresco of Sally's is going to be worth a million dollars in five years. The board won't want to be remembered as the fools who threw a bucket of paint on a million dollars." Suddenly, her face broke into a smile. "Here's the artist now."

Sally slid her arm around my waist, but her attention was directed toward Hilda. "Miss McCourt, it's wonderful to see you again. People tell me you've been my champion in all this."

Hilda McCourt beamed with pleasure. "I was happy to do it. It's always a pleasure to nudge people into acting in a civilized way. They generally want to, you know."

Sally seemed surprised. "Do they?" she said. Then she shrugged. "If you say so. Anyway, besides thanking you, I wondered if you two would let me trail around with you for a while. There's a picture here I want to see with Jo."

Hilda looked at her watch. "I think you and Joanne had better look without me. I still have choir practice to get to tonight. We're doing Charpentier's 'Midnight Mass' for Christmas. A bit of a warhorse, but a splendid piece, and I think the Southern Comfort has prepared my voice nicely."

Sally leaned forward and kissed Hilda's cheek. "Thank you again for your heroic efforts. I know Erotobiography is troubling for some people."

"Oh, I've had lovers myself," said Hilda McCourt. "Many of them," and she turned and walked across the shining parquet of the gallery floor. Her step was as light as a young girl's.

I looked at Sally. "I'll bet she has had lovers," I said. "And I'll bet she'd need a bigger wall than you have to mount her memoirs of them all."

"Right," Sally said, and she laughed. But then there was an awkward moment. I had told Hilda McCourt that Sally and I had a history. Like many histories, ours had been scarred by wounded pride and estrangement. Since I'd come to Saskatoon in July to teach at the university, Sally and I had moved carefully to establish a friendship. After thirty years of separation, it hadn't been easy, and Sally hadn't made it easier when she had suddenly left her husband and child for an affair with a student in Santa Fe.

This was the first time we had been alone together since she'd come back from New Mexico, and she seemed tense, waiting, I guess, for my reaction. In my heart, I thought what she had done was wrong, but at forty-seven I didn't rush to judgement with the old sureness any more. And I had learned the value of a friend. I turned to her and smiled.

"Now, where's this painting I can't see without you?" I said.

She looked relieved. "In Gallery II – right through that doorway."

The gallery was only yards away, but our progress was slow. People kept coming up to Sally, ostensibly to congratulate her, but really just to see her up close. She was as she always was with people, kind enough but absent. Not many of the clichés about artists were true of Sally, but one of them was: her work was the only reality for her.

"So," she said finally. "Here it is. On loan from the Art Institute of Chicago. What do you think?"

It was a painting of three people at a round picnic table: two adolescent girls in bathing suits and a middle-aged man in an open-necked khaki shirt. The man was handsome in a world-weary Arthur Miller way, and he was wholly absorbed in his newspaper. The girls were wholly absorbed in him. As they looked at him, their faces were filled with pubescent longing.

"Wow," I said. "Izaak Levin and us. That last summer at the lake. The hours we spent in the boathouse writing those steamy stories about his lips pressing themselves against our waiting mouths and about how it would feel to have him – what was that phrase we loved – lower his tortured body onto ours. Even now, my hands get sweaty remembering it. All that unrequited lust." I stepped closer to the painting. "It really is a wonderful painting, two young virgins looking for . . . What were we looking for, anyway?"

"Someone to make us stop being virgins," Sally said dryly. Then she shrugged. "And fame. Izaak was the toast of New York City in those days. Remember when he was a panelist on that TV show where they tried to guess people's jobs?" Suddenly she smiled. "Izaak's in Erotobiography, you know."

Amazingly, I felt a pang. It had been more than thirty years, but still, it had been Sally who won the prize. She'd been the one to live out the fantasy.

"Come on," she said. "I'll show you which one's his." She grinned mischievously. "Actually, maybe you could get him to show you himself. He just walked in."

"You're kidding," I said, but she wasn't. There he was across the room. Thinner, greyer, but still immensely appealing, still unmistakably the man I dreamed of through the sultry days and starry nights of that summer.

He came right over to us. Sally beamed, pleased with herself.

"Izaak, here's an old admirer," she said. "The other girl in the picture – Joanne Ellard, except now it's Joanne Kilbourn."

Izaak Levin looked into my face. His expression was pleasant but bemused. It was apparent that the only memories he had of me were connected with a piece of art Sally had made. He gestured toward it. "I've enjoyed this picture many times over the years. It's a pleasure to see that you've aged as gracefully as it has."

I could feel the blood rushing to my face. I stood there dumbly, looking down at my feet like a fifteen-year-old.

"Has your life turned out happily?" he asked.

"For the most part, very happily," I said. My voice sounded strong and normal, so I continued. "It's wonderful to see you again. Did you come up for the opening?"

He looked surprised. "I live here. This has been my home since Sally and I came back in the sixties. Didn't she ever mention it?"

"Izaak's my agent, among other things," said Sally, and then she moved closer to him and touched his arm "Incidentally, speaking of being my agent, I ran into these people in Santa Fe who bought *The Blue Horses* from you last summer. You'd better chase down the cheque because I never got it."

Her words seemed to knock Izaak Levin off base. He flushed and shook himself loose from her. "And the implication is . . . ?" he asked acidly.

"For God's sake, Izaak, the implication is nothing. I don't suspect you of financing a love nest in Miami. I've been travelling so much. I just thought the cheque must be stuck in a hotel mail slot somewhere. It's no big deal. Just track it down, that's all." She grabbed my arm. "Come on, Jo, let's go look at the filthy pictures."

There was a lineup for the Erotobiography exhibit, but we didn't wait in line. Everyone recognized Sally, and no one

seemed to mind being pushed aside. People flattened themselves against the walls to allow us safe passage. It was very
Canadian – the artist as minor royalty. And as if she were
royalty, Sally's entrance into the room transformed the
sleekly clothed art lovers from their everyday selves into
people who talked in muted voices and used significant
words: "life-affirming," "celebration," "mutability," "vari-
ability," "transcendence."

"Balls," said Sally as she moved toward the painting just
inside the door. "They have to be the hardest thing to draw.
Now look at this." The painting she pointed to was of an
intimate encounter. The woman, clearly Sally Love, sat
naked in a kind of grove while a young man knelt before her,
performing an act of cunnilingus. It was a beautiful work:
the colours were pure and vibrant, and the lines were all
curved grace. Sally reached out unselfconsciously and traced
the lines of her own painted genitals with a forefinger:
"Look how lovely a woman is – all those shapes opening up,
moistening. There are so many possibilities there, but balls
are balls – small, hard, bounding around in their crepey skin
like avocado pits or ball bearings. Just from a technical
standpoint, they were a problem – I mean to make them
individual." She looked thoughtful. "Cocks, on the other
hand, were easy. Anyway, come see."

They were three deep in front of the fresco, but the sea
parted for Sally and me, and in a minute we were standing
in front of it. The first thing that struck me was the size. It
consumed a wall about ten feet by thirty feet – huge. And
Sally had played with scale too – some of the genitals were so
large they were unrecognizable as parts of the body; they
looked like lunar landscapes, all craters and folds and folli-
cles. Some were tiny, as contained and as carefully rendered
as a Fabergé egg. The second arresting feature of the fresco
was its colour. The genitalia seemed to be floating in space,

suspended in a sky of celestial blue. I looked at those fleshly clouds and I thought how impermanent they seemed against the big blue sky, the blue that had been there before they came into being and would be there long after they were dust. People had been made miserable, yearning for those genitals; lives had been warped or enriched by them; they had made dreams become flesh and solitudes join, but isolated that way . . .

"The perspective is pretty annihilating," I said. "I don't mean in a technical sense, lust in human terms. All the agonies we go through about those little pieces of us. They look so bizarre floating up there."

Sally looked at me with real interest. "You're the first one who's picked up on that."

"And the other thing," I said, my lip suddenly curving with laughter. "Oh, God, Sally, they are funny. Did you ever see Mr. Potato Head, that toy the kids have where they give you a plastic potato and a box full of detachable parts, so you can cobble together a funny face? Well, that's what the little ones look like to me – things you'd stick into Mr. Potato Head."

"Or Mrs. Potato Head," said Sally, grinning. "Oh, Jo, what a Philistine you are. But it is so good to be with you. Sometimes I feel as if . . ."

But she never finished. A man in a leather bomber jacket had come up to us. He was slight, fine-featured and deeply tanned. He had a leather bag the colour of maple cream fudge slung over his shoulder.

"Sally, it's transcendent," he said. His voice was soft with the lazy vowels of the American South. "But, you know, pure creation isn't enough any more. Idle art is the devil's plaything. That's the new orthodoxy. We have to put Eroto-biography into a socio-political context. Be a good girl and tell me what all these dinks are saying about our social structure." He patted my hand. "You can play, too. But I get to go first. And I want to know about that wonderful pinky one at the top, second from the left."

Sally bent over and looked at the stitching on his over-the-shoulder bag. "I'll tell you that if you'll tell me where you got this. Jo, look at the needlework on this leather. Incidentally, this is Hugh Rankin-Carter; he's an art critic and an old friend."

We talked for a little while, but it was clear I was out of my league with Rankin-Carter. Besides, I was beginning to feel the effects of my Christmas Comfort, so when there was a break in the conversation, I said, "Sal, I'm going to let you two look for social context. I'm going to get something to eat."

Sally put her hand on my arm. "Don't just wander off on me, Jo. Please. At least let's make some arrangements to get together. I was going for a workout at Maggie's tomorrow. Do you want to meet me there? I'll even buy lunch."

"Sounds great," I said.

"Eleven-thirty okay with you?" she asked over her shoulder as Hugh Rankin-Carter pulled her along after him. "I'll meet you in the lobby."

A voice behind me, pleasantly husky, said, "I find it hard to believe that anyone who looks like that needs a workout."

The voice belonged to a small woman in a high-necked grey silk dress. She looked to be in her late thirties with the kind of classic good looks that grow on you: ginger hair cut boy-short, pale skin with a dusting of freckles across the nose and grey, knowing eyes. She was smiling.

I smiled back. "I think it's because she works out when she doesn't need to that she looks the way she does."

"Right," she said. "Sally Love's always been good at taking care of herself." She extended her hand. "I'm Clea

Poole. Sally and I have a gallery together – womanswork on Fourteenth Street."

"Of course," I said. "That old stone lion on your front lawn is terrific, and I love the wreath you've got around his neck for the holidays."

"Around her neck," Clea said. "It's a female lion. Anyway, sometime you should beard the lion in her den and come in and look around. We have a wonderful eco-feminist exhibition on now, Joanne – very gender affirming."

"You know my name," I said, surprised.

"Right," she said. "I know a lot of things about you. You're the other girl creaming her jeans over Izaak Levin in the lake painting."

I could feel my face grow warm. "It's a little unnerving to have your teenage lust out there for all the world to see."

"That's what Sally does – she captures the private moment."

"And makes it public?" I said.

"And makes it art," she corrected me gently. "You should be flattered."

"I guess I am," I said. "Not many people get to hang in the Art Institute of Chicago."

"Right," she said. "You're between a Georgia O'Keeffe cow skull and a Mary Cassatt mother and child."

"Great placement."

"Yes," she said seriously, "it is a great placement. Sally's the only Canadian woman artist they have."

"Another gold star for Sally."

"Right," said Clea. Then she looked at me with real interest. "I'll bet it was tough being friends with someone who got all the gold stars."

I felt myself bristling. "She didn't get them all," I said. "I've had a couple myself."

Clea Poole looked amused, and I laughed.

"Yeah," I agreed, "it was tough. I was one of those blobby ordinary little girls. Even when Sally was a beanpole of a kid, everything lit up when she walked into a room. She's always had that extra wattage."

Clea pointed across the room. Sally and Hugh Rankin-Carter were still together in front of the fresco, but they weren't alone any more. The private talk had become public. An earnest young man with a microphone was asking Sally questions, and a crowd had gathered, hushed, listening.

Clea shrugged. "As you say, extra wattage."

From across the room, a woman called Clea Poole's name. She waved, then turned to me. "I've got to get back to her. I said I wouldn't be long. But I had to meet you, Joanne. No matter how much drifting apart there was, you've always been a major player in Sally's life."

Puzzled that she knew so much about Sally and me, I watched Clea as she started to walk across the room. When she had gone a few steps, she suddenly turned.

"I'll bet Sally's tickled pink that you two are friends again," she said. I think she intended the comment to be sharp and ironic, but her tone was wistful. As she disappeared into the crush of the crowd, I thought there wasn't much doubt about the identity of the major player in Clea Poole's life.

Suddenly, I was tired of the emotional crosscurrents. I'd had enough of the art world for one evening. But there was one more drama to be played out.

The crowd in front of Erotobiography had changed. Stuart Lachlan was standing there now, and nose to nose with him was a young woman with a hand-held TV camera. Neither of them looked very happy, but the crowd watching them sure was. Stuart said something, and as the woman responded, she put down her camera and began to punch him in the chest with her forefinger. Sally, standing a little to the side, was watching the scene intently. Finally, she looked across at me. When she caught my eye, she raised two fingers to her temple in the suicide gesture I had seen her use a hundred times at school when someone was droning on too long in chapel. I smiled, and when she grinned back, I felt a rush of pleasure. As Clea Poole would say, I was tickled pink.

Despite all the Southern Comfort I'd drunk at the opening, when I crawled into bed that night, I couldn't sleep. At 2:00 a.m., wondering if Janis Joplin had had the same problem, I gave up and went downstairs. I decided on herb tea, filled the kettle and sat down at the kitchen table. The shoe box of pictures I'd hauled out that night to show my sons was still at my place. "Capezio," said the legend on the box. I remembered those shoes, soft leather dancer's shoes that had cost me a month's allowance and promised to make me graceful. The shoes had lied, and I'd pitched them out before I'd graduated from high school, but the pictures were still there.

I'd been surprised that the boys had been interested. My sons were teenagers, and knowing Sally Love wasn't exactly like knowing Darryl Strawberry before the Dodgers gave him his $20.5 million contract. But apparently being childhood friends with a woman who'd covered a wall in the Mendel Gallery with penises had a certain cachet, and after dinner that night the kids and I had had fun looking at old snapshots. There had been the usual dismissive comments about mothers in bathing suits and guys with nerd haircuts, but the pictures of Sally at thirteen had inspired reverence in my thirteen-year-old, Angus.

"Oh, she was awesome," he said, "truly awesome."

"She still is," Peter, who is eighteen, had said quietly.

In those early morning hours as I sifted idly through the pictures I realized how right the boys were. Sally had always been awesome. But the picture that stopped me wasn't one of Sally. It was one of the three of us: Sally and Nina and me. I hadn't remembered it existed. It wasn't an exceptional picture, just a faded black-and-white summer picture taken by an amateur photographer. We were in a rowboat. Sally and I were rowing, and Nina was sitting in the front. We were all smiling, waving at whoever was standing on the dock taking our picture.

"Nina and Us," it said in my handwriting on the back of the photo. And now, after thirty years of wounds and alienation and unfinished business, we were together again. It was, I thought as I went over to take the kettle off the burner, enough to make you believe in the workings of cosmic justice.

# CHAPTER

# 3

The next morning I awoke to the smell of coffee perking and bacon frying. In the kitchen my son Peter and Johnny Mathis were singing "Santa Claus Is Coming to Town." I rolled over and looked at the clock. I still had fifteen minutes before I had to get up. So I burrowed down in the warmth of my double bed and thought about my kids and Christmas.

The holidays hadn't been an easy time for my family. Four years earlier, my husband, Ian, had died in the week between Christmas and New Year's, and the year before this one I had spent the holidays recovering from an attempt to kill me that had almost succeeded. Not exactly material for a remake of *It's a Wonderful Life*.

But we had begun a new life in a new city, and I was optimistic. My sons and I had been in the house we'd rented on Osler Street since July. In the sixties, when it had been built, houses like this one had been called split-level ranchers. It was a solid house on a well-treed lot near the university. A Milton scholar who was spending a sabbatical year in England had built it himself, and apparently he had an affection for generous spaces and sunlight. In the months since we'd moved in, I'd thanked this man I'd never met a hundred times. His house had smoothed a rocky passage for me.

There were a handful of logical reasons why the move to Saskatoon, a hundred and fifty miles north of my home in Regina, had been a good idea. My two oldest children were enrolled at the university here, and the political science department had offered me a chance to teach a senior class in the contemporary politics of our province. The fact that the appointment was for one year only was, oddly enough, a plus. No commitments, no committee work, so I had time to finish the biography of the man who had been my friend and the leader of our party. Logic. But the real explanation for our coming couldn't be calibrated on a scale of reason. The year before we moved, bad things had happened in our old house, and in my bones, I had known we had to get out for a while.

As I sat listening to the cheerful, tuneless voice of my son, I smiled. This Christmas on Osler Street was going to be a good Christmas. I rolled over and pulled the blankets close. It didn't get much better than this. But as Gracie Slick used to say, "No matter how big or how soft your bed is, you still have to get out of it." It was December twenty-second, and I had things to do.

Half an hour later, when I went down to the kitchen, showered and dressed for a run, Peter was slipping eggs out of the frying pan onto a plate, and his brother was feeding his toast crusts to our dogs.

"Perfect timing," said Peter. "Two more minutes in the pan and they would have been what Dad used to call whore's eggs, black lace around the edges and hard as a rock at the centre."

"Whenever did Dad say that?" I asked.

"At the fishing camp up in Manitoba when we'd go there

with the guys. He told me not to say it in front of you because you'd think it was crude."

"Well," I said, looking at the eggs on my plate, "he was right about that. But it's a moot point. These eggs are perfect, Peter. You do know, don't you, that I've already bought all your Christmas presents?"

Peter poured me a cup of coffee. "I want to borrow your car tonight. Christy and I are going to *The Nutcracker* and it's going to be tough for us to make a grand entrance if we drive up in the king of junkers." He sat down opposite me. "One of those presents you got me wouldn't happen to be a new car, would it?"

"Nope," I said, spearing a piece of bacon, "no new car, but you can have the Volvo as soon as I'm through with it today. In the spirit of the holiday, I'll even throw in a coupon I've got for a free car wash and wax."

"Careful, Mum, those coupons don't grow on trees. When will you be finished, anyway?"

"Let's see. First, I'm going to take the dogs down to the river bank and run off this terrific breakfast. Then I'm getting a ski rack put on the car to carry the secret skis we're all getting for Christmas for our secret ski holiday at Greenwater. Then I'm going to meet Sally Love and humiliate myself at the gym. Then probably I'll come home and collapse. You can have the car by one o'clock."

"That'll be okay. Angus wants me to take him Christmas shopping. He can go to the car wash with me and vacuum out the back seat. It's really gross. He's still got Halloween candy back there."

"A mark of maturity, being able to hold on to candy for almost two months," I said to my youngest son.

He reached over and took a piece of bacon off my plate. "Oh, you couldn't eat the stuff that's back there. Most of it's got dog hair on it."

I shuddered. "I don't think I want to know about this. Let's talk about something else. How much Christmas shopping have you got left to do?"

Angus smiled innocently. "All of it."

I moved my plate toward him. "Here, have another piece of bacon. You need it more than I do."

I rinsed my dishes and put them in the dishwasher. The dogs were by the door looking at me anxiously.

"Anyone want to go for a walk?" I asked as I did every morning. As soon as I opened the drawer to get their leashes they went crazy with pleasure. They did that every morning, too. None of us liked surprises.

The morning passed happily. It was a grey day, but the dogs didn't mind, and neither did I. Along the river, there were lots of clear spaces where the brush had kept the snow off the path. It was a good day for the dogs and me to run and feel the fresh air knife at our lungs. When I stopped to look at the South Saskatchewan curling toward Lake Winnipeg, the river's cold beauty made my breath catch in my throat.

The man at the garage got the ski racks on first crack, and when I went to pay him, he smiled and said it was a Christmas present for a new customer. As I pulled into the parking lot across from Maggie's, I was filled with seasonal optimism about the human condition. It really was the time for peace on earth and good will toward one another.

Two hours later, I knew I'd peaked too soon.

The seventies gave us earth colours and macramé and places like Maggie's: private clubs where women could work out or learn about Oriental art or sit over plates piled with sprouts and talk about sisterhood. People didn't talk about sisterhood at Maggie's any more, but the food was still good, and the exercise classes were the best in the city.

Sally was sprawled over a chair in the lobby when I came in. She was wearing boots, blue jeans, a man's shirt and an old woollen jacket that looked vaguely military. Her long blond hair was loosely knotted at the nape of her neck. Over her shoulder she had slung an exquisite leather bag – the same bag that had hung over Hugh Rankin-Carter's shoulder the night before.

I leaned forward and traced a line in the stitchery. "Did Hugh Rankin-Carter earn a spot on the Wall of Fame?" I asked.

Sally grinned. "Not on my wall," she said, standing up. "He was pretty taken with Stuart, though. God, speaking of Stu, guess what I caught him doing last night at the gallery? Measuring his penis – the one on the wall. For comparative purposes, I guess," she said mildly. "Listen, class doesn't start until noon. Shall we go to the coffee shop and get in a little goof and gossip time?"

"Absolutely," I said.

The coffee shop at Maggie's was deserted. By the cash register a cardboard Mrs. Santa held up an announcement that the restaurant would be closing at noon for the staff Christmas party. The manager gave us a drop-dead look when we came in. She didn't warm to us when we refused menus and ordered a pot of Earl Grey and a bottle of mineral water.

She was back almost immediately with our order, as if to impress us with the importance of moving along quickly. But Sally wasn't in a mood to be hurried. As the woman stood behind her, Sally fished around in the new leather bag and pulled out a bottle opener and a package of rice cakes.

"Allergies." She shrugged, looking at the manager. The woman turned on her heel and left us alone.

"I'd forgotten about your allergies," I said, "or maybe I just thought you'd left them behind somewhere."

"No, I'm worse than ever. The world seems to get more dangerous every year."

I shuddered, and Sally looked at me curiously.

"No use worrying about it," she said. "I just have to be careful." She ripped the cellophane from her rice cakes. Her nails were unpolished, and her hands looked strong and capable. "Anyway, it could be worse. This doctor I saw in Santa Fe told me about a patient of his who was allergic to semen. Died on her wedding night. She started going into acute anaphylactic reaction: wheezing, gasping for air. Her husband just thought she was having this incredible orgasm, and he kept pumping away like crazy – super stud."

She held out a rice cake to me. "Here, eat. These things are guaranteed to make you live forever."

"Or make it seem like forever," I said, grimly. "God, poor woman . . . poor man. How did they figure out what happened?"

"Apparently she had a history of allergies, and Jo, when the ambulance came, the husband was sitting stark naked on the side of the bed with his weapon still smoking."

For a beat, we just looked at each other and then we both burst out laughing.

"Oh, Sal," I said, "it's so good to be together again. Now that we're in the same city, maybe we can make up for all the years we lost."

Sally reached across and patted my hand. "We'll make up for them, Jo, but not in Saskatoon. I'm not going to stick around here too much longer."

I was surprised at the sense of loss I felt, but I tried to sound philosophical. "Considering the welcome you got at the gallery last night, I can't say that I blame you."

Sally took a long sip of her mineral water. "Oddly enough I'd decided to leave before all this happened. When I approached Stu about doing the Erotobiography, I told him I wanted it to be a kind of parting gift for the city. You know I've lived here on and off for twenty-five years."

"At the moment, I don't think this city deserves a parting gift," I said.

"I've done some good work here. You know, Jo, it's going to be tough leaving. I've owned that studio on the river bank since I was twenty. Anyway, it's time. That last year I was with Stu, I made such bad art. Everything just turned grey: me, my work, the world. I wish I could buy back everything I did that year and burn it. It's so choked. You can't breathe when you look at it." She shook her head in disgust.

"I never should have married him. Stu's a nice guy and all, but he's such a stiff. I must have been crazy."

"You have Taylor," I said.

Her face brightened. "Yes, I have Taylor, and since I left Stu and that house, I'm making some decent art again. The pieces seem to be falling into place. Did you ever see that gallery I own on Fourteenth Street?"

"All the time. In fact, just last night I was telling Clea Poole how much I admire the lady lion with the Christmas wreath you've got out front."

Sally raised an eyebrow. "The lion's about the only thing worth admiring at womanswork now. The place is an embarrassment – all that seventies clitoral epiphany stuff. Clea's really lost her judgement. Anyway, there'll be something new there soon. There's a new owner."

"A new owner?" I repeated.

"Yeah, a surgeon. I got a call while I was in Santa Fe from the real estate people. They were desperate to track me down. This woman I've sold it to wants the gallery as a Christmas present for her husband. Cash. No dickering. I stopped off to sign the papers on my way in from the airport last night."

"What about Clea?" I asked. "Doesn't she have to agree to the sale?"

Sally looked puzzled for a minute. "Why? She just manages the place. I'm the owner. Anyway, it'll be good for Clea – get her out of her warm little cocoon and give her a chance to see what's happening in the big bad art world. Don't look at me like that, Jo. I've been carrying Clea Poole for twenty years. If the good doctor hadn't come along, I probably would have carried her for another twenty. But this offer came out of nowhere. It really seemed like a sign that the time had come to make some changes."

"A providential nudge?" I asked.

Sally grinned. "Yeah, that's it – a providential nudge."

"Well," I said, "Robertson Davies says it's spiritual suicide to ignore these pushes from fate."

"Sounds good to me," Sally said. "I wish Robertson Davies, whoever he is, would tell Clea I sold the gallery. When she hears about womanswork, I'd rather he was in the line of fire than me." She stood up and stretched lazily. "But that's this afternoon's problem. Right now, let's get into the gym and do it, Jo. You never know when you're going to meet the man with the smoking gun."

When Maggie's had opened, much had been made of the fact that the woman who designed the building had muted the light in the changing rooms "to forgive what we perceive as the imperfections of our bodies." As I inched my leotard on, I thought how humane that architect had been. And then I looked at Sally Love.

Naked, forty-five years old, Sally's body still didn't need forgiving. She was tanned golden everywhere, perfect everywhere. No stretch marks. No sags. No cellulite. Perfect. She pulled up her body suit and turned to me.

"Ready?" she asked.

"As I'll ever be," I said.

"So," she said, "let's get in there and shuffle it around a bit."

As soon as I walked into the gym, I knew we'd be doing more than shuffling it around. The room was filled with women whose bodies were like Sally's: sleek, hard-muscled, shining in spandex. And they all seemed younger than either of us by at least a decade.

The instructor, a tiny redhead in peppermint-striped cotton, slid a tape into her ghetto blaster and said, "This is a super-fit class, but if you can't cut it, all I ask is that you women keep moving. By the way, my name is Charlene."

I leaned across to Sally and whispered, "Did you ever notice how many aerobics instructors are named Charlene? I think it's kind of menacing."

Sally grinned and started to say something, but then the music soared and we were away.

By the time we came to the last song, an aerobic "Joy to the World," I was slick with sweat and exhausted, but Sally was glowing. On the wall of the gym were signs: "If It's the Last Dance, Dance Backwards," "You Can't Turn Back the Clock, But You Can Rewind It." As I watched Sally high kicking to the beat of the music, her blond hair tied back in a ponytail and her face set in concentration, I thought that she didn't need any inspirational signs. All on her own, she'd discovered a way to make time stand still.

When we finished our floor exercises, Sally stayed behind to do some relaxation technique she'd picked up in Santa Fe. That's how it happened that I was the first one to see Clea Poole.

She was sitting on a bench in the changing room, with her back ramrod straight and her hands folded in her lap. She was wearing a handsome grey wool coat. All around her, young women were peeling off brightly coloured body suits, laughing, gossiping; Clea in her cloth coat was set apart, a moth among the butterflies.

When I went over and said hello to her, she looked at me with dead uncomprehending eyes.

"Are you all right?" I asked.

She didn't answer.

I knelt beside her and touched her hand. "I'm Joanne Kilbourn. Remember? Sally's friend."

She pulled her hand from mine. "I remember," she said thickly. "Where's Sally?"

"She'll be along soon," I said. I waited, but Clea didn't seem to have anything to say, so I opened my locker, picked up my towel and went off to shower. When I came back, Clea was still there, sitting, waiting. She had the look of someone who would wait forever.

Sally had apparently gone straight to the showers. When she finally came in, her hair was dark with water and she had a blue towel wrapped sarong-like around her. Clea Poole jumped up and ran over to her. It seemed to take Sally a moment to focus on the situation.

"Clea, what are you doing here?"

Clea Poole's voice was tight with anger. "Where else would I be? This morning a total stranger walked into womanswork – our gallery, Sally, the one we built up together – and she told me she'd be bringing her husband around Christmas Eve to see his present." Her composure was breaking. "This person had a big red satin ribbon with her and she asked me if as a favour I'd mind tying it across the door when I closed up Christmas Eve. Sally, do you hear me? She wanted me to tie a ribbon on the front door of womanswork because you sold it to her. You sold it without telling me, Sally. Our gallery is a fucking gift for a fucking husband."

"Clea, I didn't want it to be like this. I'm sorry, truly I am, but things just happened too fast."

Clea Poole had begun to cry. As the tears spilled onto her cheeks, she wiped at them with the sleeve of her coat.

"Remember our dream about a gallery where women from all over the west could come? What am I going to do if I don't have . . ." The end of her sentence dissolved in a sob.

Sally's voice sounded tired and sad. "You're going to do what everyone else in the world does. You're going to cope. Look, Clea, it really is time for a change of direction. Nobody does all that vaginal stuff any more."

"Including you?" sobbed Clea.

"Oh, Mouse." Sally reached out to comfort Clea. The blue towel that had been wrapped around her body fell to the floor. Confronted with Sally's nakedness, Clea Poole's face grew soft. Then she bent down, picked up the blue towel and draped it over Sally's shoulders.

"I don't want you to be cold," she said simply.

It was a terrible and intimate moment. For a split second the two women stood connected but apart, then Sally enclosed Clea in her arms.

It was a ludicrous coupling: the small woman in the drab wool coat clung ferociously to Sally's naked body, as if somehow by an act of will she could penetrate that amazing Amazon beauty.

The changing room was silent except for Clea Poole's muffled sobs and Sally's voice, gentle and weary. "There, there, Mouse. It'll be all right. You'll see. It's just been a shock for you. Let me get dressed, and we'll find some place to have a quiet drink and we can talk." Her eyes swept the changing room, so carefully designed to forgive human imperfection. The air was heavy with the tension that comes after a public scene. On the pastel benches, women were hooking bras, pulling on stockings, zipping boots – trying not to be there.

Sally smiled ruefully across at me. "Thanks for coming, Jo. Let's not wait so long for the next time."

As I drove home through the snowy city streets, I couldn't shake the image of Clea Poole clinging to Sally. It was a disturbing picture. Then as I turned from Spadina Crescent onto the University Bridge my car hit an ice patch and, for a heart-stopping ten seconds, it spun lazily toward the oncoming traffic, until I gained control again. By the time I pulled into the driveway in front of my house I could feel the pins-and-needles pricks of anxiety on my skin, and I was beginning to think that maybe Sally was right. Maybe the world did get more dangerous every year.

The fear started to melt the moment I walked in the front door. The tree lights were plugged in, there was Christmas music on the radio, and my daughter, Mieka, was sitting at the dining-room table behind piles of boxes and wrapping paper and ribbons. She was wearing a green knit sweater with a bright pattern of elves and Santas, and her dark blond hair was tied back with a red ribbon. She was twenty years old and had been living with her boyfriend, Greg, in a place of their own for a year and a half, but in that moment she looked twelve, and I felt a surge of happiness that she was home and it was Christmas.

"Help," she said, "I'm three days behind in my everything."

I sat down beside her and picked up a box. "For whom? From whom?" I asked.

"For you. From me. No peeking. Now choose some nice motherly paper. Something sedate." She looked at me. "Are you okay? You look a little wiped out."

"I had a rather unsettling morning," I said, and I told her about the scene in the changing room.

When I finished, Mieka ran the edge of the scissors along a length of silver ribbon. It curled professionally and she looked thoughtful. "It sounds as if Clea/Mouse was talking about more than art. Is Sally a lesbian?"

"I don't think so . . . I think she's just someone who likes sex with an interesting partner."

"Or partners," Mieka said. She picked up a piece of red

tissue and began to wrap some baseball cards for Angus. "I went over to the Mendel this morning."

"Sally's show is turning us into a city of art lovers," I said. "So what did you think?"

"Well, the crazies were out in force. A woman stopped me on my way in from the parking lot and asked me if I was a virgin. She was pushing her dog around in a shopping cart."

"Poor dog," I said. "And poor you. Was the show worth the trip through the parking lot?"

Mieka looked up, and her eyes were shining. "Oh, Mum, it was wonderful. That fresco is the most amazing art I've ever seen. But the thing that's really dynamite is the painting of you and Sally. Of course, I had to tell everyone that was my mother up there."

"Did that impress them?"

"Stopped them dead in their tracks." Then she looked thoughtful. "The guide at the gallery told me Sally moved heaven and earth to get that painting on loan. He said that she was absolutely insistent that the lake picture be part of the exhibition so the other girl in the painting could see it." Mieka turned to me. "Did you know about it before last night?"

"No, it was a surprise. I think Sally wanted to see my reaction."

"She really must care a lot about you to go to all that trouble."

"You know," I said, "I think she does."

Mieka picked up a marker and drew paw prints on the red tissue wrapping Angus's baseball cards. She held the package up for my approval.

"Nice," I said. "The dogs are lucky to have you to wrap for them."

She smiled and handed me a box. "And I'm lucky to have you to wrap for me. It all comes around."

"Yeah," I said, "I guess it does."

For a few minutes we worked along in silence, listening to the radio. It was Mieka who spoke first.

"Mum, what happened with you and Sally? You were like sisters when you were little. You told me that yourself. But on the way back from the Mendel today, it hit me that, until you and the boys moved up here last summer, the only time I'd seen Sally was at Daddy's funeral. I remember that because afterwards, back at our house, I went upstairs and Sally and Nina were in my room fighting."

"I'd forgotten that Sally came to your dad's funeral," I said. "Of course, that day was pretty much a blur for me, I certainly don't remember a fight between Nina and Sally. What was it about?"

"I don't know," Mieka said. "It didn't matter to me. The reason I'd come upstairs in the first place was because I was starting to lose it. But I do remember hearing Nina tell Sally she should leave because all she ever did was hurt you."

"What did Sally say?"

"Nothing. I think she just left."

I picked up an Eaton's box. "What kind of paper for this one?"

"That's a pair of driving gloves for Pete – to go with the new car you're not getting him. Something manly."

I held up some shiny paper covered in toy soldiers. "Enough testosterone in this one?"

She grinned and started making a bow. "Mum, I didn't mean to pry before, when I asked you about Sally. You don't have to talk about it if you don't want to."

"Except," I said, "I think I do want to talk about it. Seeing that lake picture last night has brought back a lot of memories." I reached over and touched her hand. "Mieka, let's take a break and get some tea. I could use a daughter right now."

We sat at the table in front of the glass doors that opened onto the deck from the kitchen. The backyard was brilliant with sunshine, and at the bird feeder, sparrows were pecking through the new snow at the last of the sunflower seeds and suet I'd put out that morning.

"I don't know where to begin," I said. "Maybe when Sally's father died. That's when everything went wrong."

"September, 1958," Mieka said quietly. "The date was in the catalogue I picked up at Sally's show this morning. They had a nice little tribute to him."

"Right," I said, "except they glossed over a few things, like the way he died. Mieka, Des didn't just die. He committed suicide, and he . . . he tried to take Nina and Sally with him."

I could hear Mieka's sharp intake of breath. "He tried to kill his own wife and child?" The elves and Santas on her sweater were rising and falling rapidly. A man who could murder his family was a long way from Mieka's safe and sunny world. "He must have been a monster," she said finally.

"No," I said, "he wasn't a monster. In fact, until he got sick, he was one of the most terrific people I ever knew. I used to love just being in the same room with him. Living was so much fun for him. He was so interested in everything; he could be as passionate about the right way to cook corn on the cob as he was about the way Sally built her sand castles or the way he made art.

"Then he had this massive stroke and everything changed. He used to love to swim. When I close my eyes, I can still see him running down the hill from the cottage and diving off the end of the dock into the lake. He never hesitated. Suddenly he couldn't even walk without help. He'd been a great storyteller, and of course that was gone, too. After the stroke it was painful to watch him try to form a word. He was dependent on Nina and Sally for everything. He couldn't even feed himself properly. And, of course, worst of all, he couldn't paint. For a man who had lived every day as intensely as Des had, I guess the future just looked . . ."

"Unacceptable?" asked Mieka in a high, strained voice. "So unacceptable that he decided to kill two innocent people?"

"But he didn't kill them, Miek. My father saved Nina when he gave her the ipecac, and Sally had saved her own life by throwing up. They lived. Although for a while, I don't think they much wanted to. You know, for a time, I didn't want to. People talk about their world being turned upside-down. That was how it felt for me. As if suddenly everything had come loose from its moorings.

"That was the worst September. It rained and rained, and I was so alone and so scared. My father had to deal with everything: the police, the funeral, Nina and Sally at the hospital, his own patients. I never saw him. I remember when he came up to my room to get me for the funeral, there was a split second when I didn't recognize him. It wasn't so much that he'd aged as that life seemed to have seeped out of him. He didn't have his heart attack until that next August, but I think your grandfather started to die when Desmond Love died."

"And my grandmother was drinking," Mieka said, a statement not a question.

"Yeah, she was drinking a lot that summer, and the 'tragedy at the lake,' as the papers called it, really propelled her into the major leagues. I felt as if I didn't have anybody. Nina had always been there before, but she was in the hospital for weeks after Des died."

Mieka looked puzzled. "I thought you said she was okay."

"Physically she was, but she didn't seem to recover the way she was supposed to. I kept asking my father when I could see her and he kept saying soon, she just needed rest. I guess I believed him because I wanted to. Then one night,

I overheard my parents fighting. Your grandmother had never liked Nina and she was screaming that Nina was faking her grief, playing on my father's sympathy and my gullibility to keep us from seeing how things really had been at the lake. For once, my father didn't just let her rant. He told her that Nina had suffered a complete breakdown and he told her – oh, God, Mieka, it's been thirty years but I still feel sick when I think of this – my father said that morning when he'd gone by Nina's room on his rounds, she'd been crouched naked in the corner, tearing at her own flesh with her fingernails – like an animal in a trap, that's the phrase he used."

Across from me, Mieka winced. "It's hard to imagine. Nina's always so controlled."

"I know. Anyway, after that they were careful not to leave her alone, but I guess they didn't think Sally was in any danger. I don't know how else it could have happened, because one day Sally just walked out of the hospital. They found her with Izaak Levin."

"The man in the picture with you and Sally," Mieka said. "His name was in the show catalogue, too."

"He used to come to the cottage for a few weeks every summer. I was about to say he was a friend of Des Love's, but that wasn't the connection. Izaak was Nina's friend first. In fact, he was the one who introduced Nina to Des Love. Nina's an American, you know, from New York, and Izaak knew her there. Anyway, once Sally got to Izaak's place, she refused to leave. When my father tried to get her to come home to our house, she became hysterical. She said she was never going back to the house on Russell Hill Road. She was going to leave the city and never come back. And, of course, that's exactly what she did."

Mieka looked at me. "Sally was what? Thirteen? Why would any mother let a thirteen-year-old child move in with someone else?"

"For one thing the arrangement Nina and Izaak worked out was supposed to be temporary – just until Nina got better. There was a school of the arts for gifted children in New York, and they enrolled Sally there. She was supposed to come back at Christmas."

"Except she didn't come back at Christmas," Mieka said.

"She never came back," I said. "She never phoned. She never wrote. She just cut us all off as if we'd never existed. I must have written her a hundred letters that first year, but I never heard a word from her. Nobody did, not even Nina. She told me that Izaak kept her informed about Sally's progress, but she never heard a word from her own daughter."

Mieka looked puzzled. "Why would Nina let the situation go on? Can you imagine letting me just walk out of your life when I was thirteen?"

I smiled at her. "I can't imagine letting you walk out of my life ever. But that's us. Nina and Sally always had difficulties. When I think about it now, a lot of it was Des. He loved Sally so much and, of course, he was her teacher as well as her father. I think sometimes Nina must have felt excluded."

"All the same, Sally was Nina's daughter," Mieka said.

"It was a bad time for everybody," I said. "And in bad times, people don't always think clearly. It must have been hard for Nina to know what was best for Sally, because no one could really understand why she'd turned against us. My dad's explanation was that Sally was so filled with rage at Des for leaving her that her feelings for everyone and every place connected with him were tainted."

Mieka looked thoughtful. "That makes sense to me. Don't forget, Mum, she was only a kid. Thirteen – the same age as Angus is now. That's pretty young to think things through."

"Oh, Mieka, I know. But then the next year, when your grandfather died, Sally didn't even come to the funeral. Izaak

Levin came, but he said Sally refused to come to Toronto. He had to leave her with his sister in New York. For a long time I found it hard to forgive her for that. My dad would have done anything for Sally, and she must have known how much I needed her. If I hadn't had Nina, I don't know if I could have made it."

Mieka's face was sad, "Did you ever hear Sally's side of the story?"

"No, I never did. When Sally and I finally got together again last summer, we were both pretty careful not to bring up the past. But I'm beginning to wonder now if that wasn't a mistake. There's a part of me that's still mad at her, you know. And that's not fair to either of us."

"Talk to her," Mieka said simply.

I stood up. "Well, doctor, if the therapy session's over, we'd better get back to our wrapping. But come here and let me give you a hug first – for being so smart. I'll throw in dinner, too, if you want. I think I've got a pan of lasagna in the freezer."

She stood up and stretched. "Sounds good. I'll consider it a professional fee. And, Mum, don't forget to hear Sally's side of things. I think after all this time, it may finally be her turn."

# CHAPTER

# 4

On the morning before Christmas I was pouring myself a second cup of coffee and thinking about making French toast for breakfast when the phone rang. Until the night of Sally's opening, I hadn't heard that low, gravelly voice for thirty years, but I knew who it was immediately. You don't forget anything about a man you dreamed about through the heat-shimmering days and moonlit nights of your sixteenth summer.

Izaak Levin's invitation had the polish that only practice brings. "Joanne, forgive the early morning call please, but in all the excitement the other night I didn't have a chance to make an arrangement to see you again. I know this is Christmas Eve, and I'm sure you have plans, but I thought perhaps between Christmas and New Year's we could have dinner together and share our remembrance of things past."

"That sounds wonderful," I said, "but my kids and I are going to Greenwater to ski that week. Can I have a rain check?"

"Of course," he said. "I'll call early in the new year. I won't let you slip away again . . ."

As I hung up, I could feel my face flush. There was a mirror on the wall above the phone, and I gave myself a hard, critical look. My hair was the same ashy blond it had always been, but now it took more than lemon juice and sunshine to keep it that way. There were fine lines in the skin around my eyes, and my face was fuller than it had been when I was young, but, on the whole, I was comfortable enough with what I saw. "Not Sally Love, but not bad," I said to my reflection. "Izaak Levin would be a fool to pass you up this time." When the phone rang again, I was still smiling.

The smile didn't last long. Sally was on the line, sounding edgy but in control.

"Jo, somebody just called to tell me there was a fire last night at womanswork. I should go down and see how bad the damage is. Would you come with me?" There was silence for a moment and when she spoke again, her voice had lost its authority. "I really could use some company, Jo. Can you meet me there in half an hour?"

"I'll be there," I said.

I went upstairs, dressed in a heavy wool sweater and jeans, woke Peter to tell him I'd be back before lunch, started out the door, then came back and made Peter come downstairs. "In case of a fire," I said, vulnerable again.

When I backed the car out of the garage, it was snowing, theatrical lacy flakes that drifted steadily through the December air and made the city look like a scene from an old Andy Williams Christmas special. It was a little after eight-thirty, and the traffic was light as I drove across the bridge toward the centre of the city.

Fourteenth Street was a pretty street of pre-war houses, restored and fitted out as offices for architects and fast-track law firms; womanswork was in the middle of the block. What I remembered was a two-storey grey clapboard building, simple and elegant. It wasn't elegant any more, but as I looked through the smoky, snowy haze at what had once been Sally's gallery, I was struck by the fact that even the ruins of the building had a certain perverse beauty. Water from the fire hoses had frozen in fantastic patterns against the charred skeleton, and snow had begun to layer itself on the burned wood. When I squinted against the smoke, the gallery looked like a Christmas gingerbread house.

It didn't take long to spot Sally. She was standing in what had once been the front door to the gallery talking to a firefighter. She was wearing the Navajo blanket coat she'd worn the night of the opening, and its purple, turquoise, orange and blue were a splash of brilliance in the grey. She came over as soon as she saw me.

"Arson," she said. "At least that's what they think. I'm supposed to come up with a list of my enemies. Maybe I should just give them the Saskatoon phone book and a pin." She sounded as strong and defiant as ever, but when she raked her hand through her hair, I noticed her fingers were trembling. Up close, her face looked drawn despite its tan. There was a smudge of soot under her cheekbone. I reached out and rubbed it with my mitt.

She smiled. "Oh, God, Jo, I feel awful. I need a five-mile run or a stiff drink."

I looked at my watch. "It's nine o'clock straight up. I think the sun must be over the yardarm somewhere. Come on, let's get out of here."

As we started toward our cars, I heard a shout behind us. It was the young firefighter Sally had been talking to. He ran up and handed something to her.

"I thought maybe this might have some sentimental meaning for you," he said.

Suddenly the wind picked up, and as the three of us stood looking down at what he had brought, the snow swirled around us. It was a porcelain doll, obviously old. Not much was left of her clothes, and her hair had been burned so that only a scorched frizz shot out around her face. But her face was intact, and her eyes, as fiercely blue as Sally's own, looked up defiantly out of the sooty porcelain.

Sally slid the doll through the opening between the top buttons of her coat so that it rested against her chest, then she leaned over and kissed the firefighter on the cheek.

"Thanks," she said, and she started to walk across the lawn toward the street. I looked at the young man standing in the snow, transfixed. Sally was old enough to be his mother, but the look on his face wasn't the kind of look a man has after his mother kisses him.

"Dream on," I said under my breath, and then I put my hands in my pockets and ran through the snow to catch up with Sally.

She wanted to go back to her studio on the river bank. I said I'd follow her. The streets were clogged with snow and last minute shoppers, so it was after nine-thirty when I pulled up behind Sally in front of her place on Saskatchewan Crescent.

She called it a studio, but really it was a one-storey bungalow on a fashionable street of pricey older houses. Years before, Sally had torn down walls and opened the house up with windows and a skylight so that her work area would look out on the river.

When we opened the front door, the house was cold and the air smelled of paint and turpentine and being closed up. There was a tarp thrown down in the centre of the room, and it was covered with containers of paint: tins, buckets, plastic ice-cream pails, jam jars. There were canvases stacked against a wall and a trestle table with brushes and boxes of pencils and rags and lengths of wood and steel that looked like rulers but were unmarked. In the corner farthest from the window were a hot plate, a couple of open suitcases and a sleeping bag.

"*La vie bohème*," I said.

Sally looked around as if she were seeing the room for the first time. "I guess it is a little depressing," she said, "but my living here is just temporary. Although," she said gloomily, "with this fire, I'm probably going to be stuck here till fucking forever. You know, Jo, I don't even know if womanswork was still mine last night. There was a possession date on the papers I signed, but who pays attention to stuff like that?"

"Well," I said, "I'll guarantee there's a surgeon in town who's paying a lot of attention to stuff like that at this very minute. A burned-out building isn't much of a Christmas present. Anyway, I think the first order of business is to call your lawyer and your insurance agent."

The phone was in the corner by the sleeping bag. Sally dropped to her knees and swept aside a pile of clothes that covered her answering machine.

"Jo, look at this. I was working last night and I always just turn off the phone and leave the machine on. I plugged the phone back in when I went to bed but I didn't check my messages." Over the red light signalling that there had been a call was a little window with digital numbers recording the number of messages received. The number in the window was sixty-two.

"It must be a mistake," I said.

Sally hit the play button. "Let's see," she said.

A computerized voice announced the date and time of the first message: December 23, 9:05 p.m. Then Stuart Lachlan's voice, tight and strained, was telling Sally that Christmas dinner would be served at two o'clock, but if she wanted to come and see Taylor's presents, she was welcome at one-thirty.

"You're a wild man, Stu," said Sally, and she pushed herself up off the sleeping bag and walked across the room to the table where she'd thrown her coat. She picked up the porcelain doll and started checking solvents on her work-table. The computer voice announced call number two at 9:30 P.M. With a start, I recognized Izaak Levin's voice, but there was none of that easy charm I'd heard an hour before. He was telling Sally he had to talk to her immediately. His voice sounded urgent. Five minutes later, when he called back with the same message, he sounded menacing. The fourth call came at 10:03. It was Clea Poole; her voice was husky, heavy with emotion, again apologizing – she tried to laugh at that word – for the scene at Maggie's. But she immediately began to replay the scene, and she was cut off in mid-sentence when the time for her message ran out. She called again, within seconds, picking up where she had left off. Throughout the night, her litany of betrayal and longing had continued. In all, there were fifty-nine calls from Clea. Sometimes the interval between calls was half an hour; sometimes there were three or four calls in a row. At the end, her voice, dead from pain and exhaustion, was as void of emotion as the mechanical computer voice that announced the time of her calls.

All the while Clea talked, Sally worked on the doll, cleaning its face and body, dabbing at its burned frizz of hair with some kind of cream and then taking a scarf that she had obviously brought back from Santa Fe and cutting it into a sarong and turban. When the machine clicked, signalling there were no more messages, Sally turned toward me and held up the porcelain doll. With her frizz of hair shining from the cream and her Carmen Miranda outfit, she looked sensational.

"What do you think?" Sally asked.

"I think you saved the doll. Saving Clea Poole is going to be harder. Sally, she needs help, and so do you. I think you should take that tape to the police."

Sally shook her head impatiently. "I can't do it, Jo."

"For God's sake, why not? I wouldn't be surprised if Clea set the fire herself. She's clearly over the edge."

"Who pushed her?" asked Sally. "Damn, I don't even know what made me sell womanswork. I don't need the money. It was just some symbolic thing – good-bye to all that. Case closed. Now Clea's frying her brain about it."

She reached over and switched on the radio. The Christmas weather forecast was snow and more snow. Sally listened for a moment, then she said quietly, "Jo, you can't push somebody over the side of a cliff and then be surprised when they fall. I won't take the tape to the cops. It's not that I don't think you're right about Clea. Burning down a building she loved is just the kind of thing she'd do. She's big on symbolism. You know she used to have the most beautiful hair. It was a coppery red colour and long. She hadn't cut it since she was a kid. Anyway, when I married Stu, Clea had a kind of breakdown, and she hacked off her hair and mailed it to us at the house."

"Oh, Sally, how awful. Poor Clea. I can't imagine that kind of mourning. It can't have been much fun for you and Stu, either."

Sally shook her head. "No, it wasn't. And there were phone calls then, too. Hundreds of them. Just like these. Stu was going to go to the police, but I told him not to. I took Clea to the desert with me for a couple of weeks. When we came back, she was okay again.

"Anyway, the buildings of Saskatoon are safe. Clea's a one-trick pony, and she's done her trick. I'm not going to turn her in to the police. But I'm not going to stay here and dry her tears, either. As soon as the holidays are over, I'm going to take my daughter and go someplace hot where nobody knows me."

I was astounded.

"Take Taylor? Where did that come from? I thought you and Stu had agreed to leave Taylor with him. At least that's what Nina told me."

"That was the arrangement before Nina came into the picture. Don't look at me like that, Jo. Let's just say I've changed my mind. I want to show you something." She took a framed drawing off the wall by the trestle table and handed it to me.

It was a picture drawn on paper with felt pens. In it a row of hula dancers with spiky eyelashes and corkscrew shoulder-length curls bumped grass skirts against one another. It was indisputably a child's picture, but even I could see evidence of real skill and something that went beyond skill.

When I looked up, Sally was still focused on the drawing. Her face was soft with love and pride. "Look at that, Jo. It's exciting all over. There's something interesting going on everywhere on that paper. You'll have to take my word for it. It's an exceptional picture for a child of four. If it weren't, if all her pictures weren't so good, I'd tell Nina to take a hike and I'd leave Taylor with Stu."

Mother love. I didn't know what to say, and so I said nothing. My silence spurred her into uncharacteristic self-justification.

"It would be immoral to leave her in that house, Jo. I know I can't expect you to understand, but if Taylor is going to make art, she can't have someone standing around telling her what it means all the time. You know what Stu used to do? He'd come over here when I was working and give me all these insights about my work and then sit back and wait for praise – like a dog bringing me a dead bird." Her voice dropped into a deadly imitation of Stuart Lachlan's. "'You see, don't you, Sally, that your art invites judgements that are sexually dimorphic: women judge its complex inter-relationships; men look to its statement.'"

In spite of myself, I laughed. "God, you and Nina, you're both so good at mimicking. I was always afraid you did imitations of me behind my back."

Sally smiled. "I'd never mock you, Jo, and Nina thinks you walk on water. Of course, she'd never make fun of her Stuart, either. She's right. He's a good person. It's just – he's dangerous to be around when you're working. He'd wall Taylor in with words, Jo, and the art she made would get more airless and miserly till he choked her off altogether."

"Have you told him?" I asked.

"I thought I'd tell him tomorrow."

"On Christmas Day! Come on, Sally."

"Okay, Jo, you win. But soon. I don't like putting things off. Now come on, get out of here. I'm all right now, and it's the day before the big event – you must have a million things to do. Here," she said, and she handed me the porcelain doll, "souvenir of your morning."

I took the doll, put on my coat and boots and walked to the door. When I opened it, the winter light hit Sally full in the face. She looked tired and somehow forlorn.

Stuart Lachlan didn't know that his estranged wife planned to take their daughter. If he had, I would have suspected him of staging the paean to family life that my kids and I walked into that Christmas Eve. On the front lawn of the Lachlan house on Spadina Crescent, there were three snow people: a father, a mother and a little snow girl. They all had pink scarves, and the snow lady had a pink hat and purse; the snow girl was holding up a sign: "Merry Christmas from Taylor."

Taylor herself opened the door to us. She was dressed like a child in a Christmas catalogue, all velvet and lace. Her hair, which was blond and thick, like Sally's, had been smoothed into a sleek French braid. Taylor's hair may have been like her mother's, but her face, fine-boned, dark-eyed and grave, was Stuart Lachlan's. She thanked us for the gifts we had brought, placed them carefully on a sea chest that was covered with a piece of Christmas needlepoint and disappeared down the hall.

"I'll bet you a vat of bath oil that she's forgotten all about us," said Mieka.

"No, that was your trick," I said. "All those kids in snowsuits, melting in the front hall when you went upstairs for a pee and forgot about them. Taylor seems to have better long-term memory than you had."

"A tuna fish sandwich has better long-term memory than Mieka has," said Peter as he hung up his coat and walked into the living room.

Angus followed him, looking around. "Deadly," he said, and he was right. Royal Doulton Santas gleamed, expensive and untouchable, behind the glass of a curio case; teak camels, big as rocking horses, strolled behind intricately carved wise men carrying gold, frankincense and myrrh to the baby king. On the mantel above the fireplace, real holly filled pink Depression-ware pitchers, and antique wooden blocks spelled out the names of the people in that household for Santa: Taylor, Daddy, Nina, and then, a little apart, Sally.

Mieka and I took off our things and followed the boys into the living room.

"You know," I said, "every year I promise myself we're going to have a living room that looks like this for Christmas, and every year I end up hauling out the same old decorations. The only thing I ever seem to change is the poinsettias."

"I like the way our living room looks," said Peter, "but if you want something different, one of the guys in my biology lab showed me a battery-operated Santa Claus he got at the Passion Pit. Mum, you should see the stuff that Santa can do, and just with four double-A batteries."

I was just about to ask for details when I heard Stuart Lachlan's voice behind me.

"Oh, good, you've made yourselves at home." He was standing in the living-room doorway. Beside him, her hand gripping his, Taylor smiled tentatively. Stu came in and kissed my cheek.

"Sorry we weren't here to greet you, but we had a little problem in the kitchen. Nina's taking care of it."

"Then," I said, smiling back at him, "it's taken care of. There's never been a problem yet that Nina couldn't vanquish."

As if on cue, Nina appeared in the doorway, flushed and laughing. "Jo has always been my one-girl fan club."

"No longer a girl," I said, "but still a fan. Nina, you look beautiful." And she did, although it was a risky look. Her hair was smoothed into a French braid, not as long as Taylor's, but I could see the intent had been to suggest relationship, and Nina's dress was the same dusky rose as her granddaughter's. It was a stunning outfit. The dress itself was very plain, high-necked and long-sleeved, but over the dress, she had a white organdy apron, full in the skirt, fitted in the bodice and gently flaring over each shoulder. Stunning, but a bit self-consciously domestic.

As she had been all my life, Nina was quick to read my expression. "I know, Jo, the apron is a tad too lady-of-the-manor, but an hour ago the roof of Taylor's gingerbread house slid to the floor and smashed, so I just made a replacement."

Not in that outfit, I thought, but it was such an innocent subterfuge, and Nina looked so happy, I couldn't help smiling. "It's a beautiful dress, Ni, and I notice it matches your granddaughter's. Pink must be the colour of choice on Spadina Crescent this Christmas."

"It's Taylor's favourite," said her grandmother simply.

"Now, Stuart, why don't you get us drinks." She touched the little girl's shoulder. "And Taylor and I will get our special cookies."

Stuart came back with a tray full of soft drinks for the children and a bottle of Courvoisier for the adults. When Angus saw the soft drinks, he was jubilant.

"Great," he exclaimed. "None of that crappy eggnog. Everywhere you go people give you that stuff, and it's so gross."

When Nina appeared in the doorway with a cut-glass bowl of eggnog, Peter turned to his brother. "Way to go, Angus," he said.

"I can dress him up, but I can't take him anywhere," I said, laughing. Taylor came in, carefully balancing a plate of cookies.

"Why?" she asked, and in the set of her mouth I could see the girl who had told a classmate to lay off Sally because *his* mother had a mustache. "Why can't you take him anywhere?"

"Because he always acts silly," I said. "Those cookies are beautiful, Taylor. How did you make the ones with the little stars cut out on top?"

Gravely and in great detail Taylor gave me the recipe, then she told me how she and her grandmother had made the candy-cane cookies, twisting pink and white together, and the gingerbread Santas with the red sugar hats and the beards white with icing. As she explained, her dark eyes never left my face, just as Stuart's eyes never left your face when he was trying to make you understand something.

"These cookies really take me back," I said to Nina, "especially the jam-jams with the little stars. You must have spent a hundred hours making those with me when I was little."

"You always dropped the cookie dough on the floor at least four times," said Nina. "All those dirty little cookies."

"But always miraculously perfect when they came out of the oven. How did you do that Nina, smoke and mirrors?"

"No," she said, laughing, "more domestic than that. I always had an extra batch of dough in the refrigerator. I still do. Sometimes grown-ups have to intervene, you know, for everybody's good." She turned her perfect heart-shaped face to me and smiled conspiratorially. "While we're being nostalgic, come upstairs with me and let me show you what I'm giving Taylor for Christmas."

When we came to the guest room that Nina was using during her visit, I was surprised to see her take down a key from the molding over the door.

"A bit Gothic novel, I know," she said, "but I'm a believer in Christmas secrets. Now you close your eyes, too. I want to see your face when you see Taylor's present." She led me into the room. "All right, Jo, you can look now."

When I opened my eyes, I was back forty years in the brick house Sally and Nina and Desmond Love had lived in on Russell Hill Road in Toronto. On Nina's night table, faces carefully painted into expressions of gentility, were those emblems of nineteenth-century womanhood, Meg, Jo, Amy, Beth, and Marmee from Louisa May Alcott's *Little Women*. An American dollmaker had produced the dolls in the late 1940s. The woman's name was Madame Alexander, and the dolls had become famous. Nina had gone to New York especially to buy a set for Sally's fifth birthday.

"I see you replaced Amy," I said.

"Yes," said Nina, straightening the ribbon on the Marmee doll's hair.

A memory. A room full of little girls in party dresses and patent leather shoes, clustered around the dolls, watching. And Nina with that same gesture. "You see, this is Marmee, the mother doll. She's a mother like me, and these are her girls. This one with the brown eyes and the strawberry blond hair is Meg. She's the oldest, and this one with the brown hair and the plaid rickrack on her petticoat is Jo – she likes to read, like our Jo does, and this is Amy, she's Marmee's little artist, like you, Sally, and she has beautiful blond hair just like . . ."

But Sally wasn't listening any more. Her face dark with fury, she grabbed the Amy doll by the ankles and smashed her china face against the edge of the table. Her voice had been shrill with hysteria. "She is not me. I am my own Sally Love," and she'd hurtled blindly past all her birthday guests and out of the room.

In this room, now, Nina was talking. "Yes. I replaced her, and she cost a small fortune, but Taylor's worth it. She's such a bright little girl, and she's like you were, Jo; she wants to learn. It's fun to do things for her. She's going to grow up to be a beautiful and gracious woman."

"Like her grandmother," I said.

Nina's face shone with happiness. "Thank you, Jo. That means a lot. Everyone needs to feel valued. I haven't had enough of that feeling lately." She shrugged. "But no self-pity. It's Christmas. And I have wonderful things to look forward to in the new year." She took both my hands in hers. "Come on, let's sit down for a minute. I have some news."

We sat down facing one another on the edge of her bed. I could smell the light flowery scent of her perfume. Always the same perfume – Joy. "A woman's perfume is her signature, Jo." That's what she'd told me. The glow from the lamp on the night table enclosed us in a pool of yellow light, shutting out the darkness.

"Stuart's asked me to move here permanently," she said. "When I came, we'd agreed to try the arrangement until Sally came to her senses, but I think we all know that's not going to happen. Stuart thinks Taylor needs a mother or at least someone to take the place of a mother in her life. Jo, it took me three seconds to give him my answer. I've put my house in Toronto on the market. It looks as if you and Stuart are stuck with me."

I felt my heart sink. "That's great news," I said weakly.

Puzzled, Nina looked at me. "I thought you'd be thrilled, Jo. I know I was, at the thought that after all these years, you and I'd be in the same city again, able to pick up the phone and meet for lunch or tea or go for a walk."

"I am thrilled," I said. "One of the best Christmas gifts I could have would be having you here permanently. It's just . . . has anyone thought about what Sally might want in all of this?"

"Sally always thinks enough about Sally for all of us," Nina said sharply. "Damn it, Jo, she made her decision when she walked out on Stuart and Taylor. She didn't go alone you know. She went with a student of hers, a boy of seventeen. It didn't last, of course. Do you know the joke that went around the gallery? 'Someone told Sally Love it was time she thought about having another child. So she went out and had herself a seventeen-year-old boy.' You should have seen Stuart's face the first time he heard that. He came home looking like a whipped dog. No, Jo, we haven't given much thought to Sally in all this, or perhaps I can put it more acceptably, we've given her about as much thought as she gave us." Her face, usually so expressive, was a mask.

I reached out to embrace her, and she turned away. "Nina, don't," I said. "Don't be angry at me."

She took my hands in hers again. "I could never be angry at you, Jo."

"And don't be angry at Sally. She wants what's best for Taylor, too. And she has her own worries right now. Did you hear her gallery burned down last night?"

"Of course. It was all over this evening's paper. Stu thinks it must have been some sort of retaliation for Erotobio-graphy. Sally's always chosen to live on the edge, Jo. And if you live on the edge, you have to accept consequences. I'm just glad she's out of this house. It wouldn't have been much of a Christmas for Taylor being stalked by a lunatic." She stood up and smoothed her hair. "I don't want to talk about this any more. Come on, let's go downstairs. We have one last Christmas Eve surprise."

We came back to a scene of perfect holiday harmony. The boys and Stu were sprawled on the floor in front of the fireplace looking at baseball cards, and Mieka and Taylor were sitting side by side at the coffee table, drawing butterflies.

It was Nina who broke the spell.

"All right, Taylor," she said. "Time to come into the dining room for the big moment."

"The next event calls for champagne," Stuart said, filling five glasses and splashing two more. "Now you Kilbourns stand right there in front of the French doors, and I'll go back into the dining room and let you know when we're ready."

The kids and I stood obediently, with that self-conscious air of celebration that comes when you're holding a glass of champagne. Someone turned off the lights; the doors to the dining room were flung open, and we were confronted with the extravagance of the Lachlan family Christmas tree.

It was a plantation pine, full and ceiling high; its fragrant, soft needles had the fresh green of new growth, but everything else was pink. There were dozens of dusty pink velvet bows tied to the branches, and each of them held a shining pink globe. And there were candles, pink, lit candles that sputtered a fatal hairbreadth away from pine needles, and there were pink roses, real ones suspended from the pine branches in tiny vials of water that glistened in the candlelight. Beside the tree, Stu and Nina and Taylor stood, hands linked. "We wish you a merry Christmas," they sang in their thin, unprofessional voices, and I felt a sense of dread so knife-sharp it sent the room spinning.

"Steady," Peter said, and I felt his arm around my shoulder. The moment passed, and in seconds, we were all drinking champagne and exclaiming over the tree.

Twenty minutes later, Taylor's stocking hung with care and the last holiday embraces exchanged, the children and I were walking along the river bank toward the Cathedral of St. John the Divine. The church was packed, and we had to sit on a bench at the back. Beside us Mary, Joseph and a real baby sat waiting for their cue. I knew the girl playing Mary. She had borrowed our tape recorder at the beginning of school and gone out to the dump to do a project on all the reusable things people throw out. The local TV station had heard about it, and I'd seen her on the evening news, standing on a mountain of garbage, swatting at flies and telling us that time was running out for the environment. A real firebrand. At the front of the church a boy in a white surplice and Reeboks started to sing "Once in Royal David's City" and Mary stood up, adjusted her baby, shook Joseph's comforting arm off her shoulder and strode up the centre aisle. A Mary for our times.

It was a good service. Hilda McCourt had been right about the beauty of Charpentier's "Midnight Mass" for Christmas, and as we left St. John the Divine's, I felt happy and at peace. The anxiety that had been gnawing at me since Nina told me about her plans to move to Saskatoon was gone. That night when, stockings filled and breakfast table set, I finally crawled into bed, I fell into an easy sleep.

But not an untroubled one. Sometime in that night I dreamed a terrible dream. I was in Stuart Lachlan's house, and Sally was there with me. There was a Christmas tree with candles, and Sally was lighting them, very carelessly thrusting a lighted taper in among the branches. I kept pleading with her to be careful, but she just laughed and said, "It's not my problem." With the terrible inevitability of a dream, the tree caught fire, and as I looked through the burning branches, I could see Nina's face. My legs were leaden, but finally, blinded by smoke, I pushed through the fire to get to her. Then we were outside somewhere and I was holding Nina, but it was dark and I was frantic because I couldn't see if she was all right. Finally, I put her down in the snow, crouched beside her and lit a match. But the face on the woman in the snow wasn't Nina's. It was Sally's. Her clothes had burned away, and her wonderful blond hair was just a charred frizz around her face, but her open eyes were still bright with defiance. And that was a strange thing because I knew she was dead.

# CHAPTER

# 5

When I opened my eyes Christmas morning, the porcelain doll Sally had given me was on my nightstand looking back at me. I must have left it there when I'd gone to wash my hair after I got back from womanswork. That morning as I looked into the doll's bright, unseeing eyes, it seemed as if my dream of fire and death had been carried over into the waking world, and I was uneasy. But after I'd showered and dressed, I felt better. It had, after all, been only a dream.

When I went downstairs, the kids were sitting in the living room trying to be cool about the fact that there were presents under the tree and it was Christmas morning. As soon as he saw me, Angus called out the name on the first present, and in the usual amazingly short time, the room was filled with empty boxes and wrapping paper and ribbons and it was over for another year.

Around noon, I called Sally's studio. There was no answer, and I felt edgy. But when Nina called early in the afternoon to wish us happiness, she said Sally was sitting in their living room, and I stopped worrying. We ate around five. Peter's girlfriend, Christy, had spent the day with us, and when we came in from cleaning up the kitchen, the boys were already taking down the tree.

"Oh," Christy said, "it seems so soon."

"We're leaving after breakfast tomorrow. There won't be anybody here to look at it," Peter said, and he began wrapping the lights around a cone of newspaper. "A woman on *Good Morning, Canada* showed how to do this," he said. "It's supposed to keep them from getting tangled."

"I've certainly tangled enough in my time," I said.

He smiled. "It's because you don't watch enough television." Then he looked up. "It was a great Christmas wasn't it, Christy?"

I looked at her standing in the doorway. She was wearing a Christmas sweatshirt under a pair of red overalls, and she was flushed with happiness. I expected her to answer him with her usual headlong rush of superlatives, but she looked at me and said simply, "It was the best Christmas I ever had," and I could see why Peter was beginning to care so much for her.

"Pete," I said, "be a good guy and show Christy and me how to make those paper cones. I hate it when you kids know more than I do."

The next morning as we started for Greenwater everybody was in a rotten mood. Mieka and Greg had almost cancelled because Greg was coming down with a cold; Peter was angry because, at the last minute, Christy had decided to go to Minneapolis with friends instead of coming north with us. Angus was worrying about the dogs languishing at the vet's, and I was worrying because everybody was so miserable. To top it all off, the weather had warmed up dramatically.

When I went out to the car for a last-minute check, Pete was clicking the new skis into the rooftop carrier.

"I wonder if we're even going to need these," he said gloomily.

I looked around. The sun was shining hard, and patches of snow on our front lawn were already fragile, melting, blue under white.

"Of course we'll need them," I said. "This is Saskatchewan. We'll need skis, and before the week's out, we'll need raincoats, and we'll probably even wish we'd brought our bathing suits along." I ruffled his hair. "This is God's country. Have a little faith, kid."

He was just beginning to smile when Angus came barrelling through the front door saying Sally was on the phone.

As I went inside, I felt oddly relieved. I picked up the receiver.

"So," I said, "how was your Christmas?"

"It was a real jingle bell," she said. "How long have you got?"

"The kids are packing up the car. About five minutes."

"Okay, in five minutes. First, I didn't take your advice. Couldn't wait to break the news to Stu that I wanted to take Taylor. I told him right after we ate. Lousy timing in that mausoleum with that tree straight out of decorator hell." Her voice dropped. "Honestly, Jo, what did you think of that tree?"

"I thought it was a little excessive."

On the other end of the phone, she mimicked my words. "'A little excessive.' Oh, yes, indeed. Anyway, I should have waited till Stu was alone because there was Nina giving him massive infusions of backbone and making subtle remarks about the problems I bring on myself because of my questionable lifestyle and my odd friends."

"Come on, Sal," I said. "Be fair here. There *are* problems, and Nina's stepped right into the middle of them. She's doing the best she can."

For a minute Sally's irony vanished. "Jesus, Jo, are you ever going to wake up to that woman?" Then she laughed. "Okay, okay, I withdraw that. I don't want you mad at me, too. You're the only sane person I know. Clea seems to be in deep waters again. Last night Stu caught her in the bushes in front of his house with a video camera whirring away. I think I'm going to have to do something about her, after all."

"Sally, be careful. Clea sounds as if she's beyond a woman-to-woman chat; you might just do her more harm than good. She needs professional help."

"Who doesn't?" Sally said grimly. "Maybe we can find a shrink who'll give us a group rate. I could use a little under-standing myself. I'm beginning to think the world has declared open season on Sally Love. I haven't finished telling you about my Christmas. The battle with Stu and Nina was just for openers. When I came back to the studio, there was this box on my doorstep – all wrapped in shiny paper, very pretty and Christmassy. So I took it inside and opened it – it was full of used sanitary napkins. There was a note saying that since I seemed to like filth . . . well, you get the idea."

"Oh, Sally, no!"

"Look, let's be grateful. It didn't explode or bite. Hold on, there's more. I took my little prezzy out to the trash, and when I came back in, Izaak was slumped against my front door, full of the Christmas spirit and about a quart of Scotch. He spent last night here, passed out on my sleeping bag. But I wasn't lonely because Clea was lurking around out front all night with her Brownie." She was laughing, but it sounded awful to me.

"Sally, why don't you give yourself a break. Go to a hotel for a few days, or better yet, we're going to be out of this house in twenty minutes. Come and stay here away from every-thing. You can take care of whatever business you have to deal with during the day and get some peace at night. The dogs are already at the kennel, so you won't even have them to bug you. And we're both past the stage where a sleeping bag is an adventure. Wouldn't it be nice to sleep in a real bed?"

"Would it ever," she said wearily. "You've got yourself a houseguest. Leave the keys in the mailbox."

"They'll be there," I said. "Have fun. And I'm sorry about your Christmas. Next year will be better."

"Promise?" she said.

"Promise," I said, and hung up.

As soon as we arrived in Greenwater, the cloud that had been hanging over us seemed to vanish. Greg's cold didn't materialize. Peter and Angus snapped out of their funks, and the temperature dipped. The skies were clear; the sun shining through the tree branches made antler patterns on the snow, and the ski trails were hard packed and fast.

Every morning we woke to birdsong, the smell of last night's fire and the bite of northern cold. Our days developed a pattern. As soon as we cleaned up after breakfast, we'd cross-country ski. When we got tired, we'd hike the nature trails and Angus would read the small metal plates that told us what we were seeing: beaver dams, aspen stands, places where carpenter ants had made their intricate inlay on tree trunks and fallen branches.

"Think of a world without decay," he would read in his serious, declaiming voice. "Think of it. Every animal that died and every tree that fell would lie there forever. Decay is essential to the recycling of energy and nutrients through successive generations of organisms."

At noon, we'd go back to the cabin, and Mieka and I would make a fire and the boys would make soup in the old white and blue enamelled cooking pot. After lunch, we'd dry our boots in front of the fire and argue lazily about whether we'd

ski in the afternoon or skate or just take the binoculars and
a bag of peanuts and look for squirrels and birds.

We'd eat early, and by seven o'clock I'd be in my room
working on my book about Andy Boychuk and trying to
block out the sounds of the kids laughing and fighting over
cards or Monopoly. By ten o'clock we'd all be in bed. The
good life.

Until the last day of the old year, the day we left
Greenwater, I felt immune to the ugly things that life sometimes coughs up. Then the immunity ended.

I'd given my two guys and Mieka's Greg new hockey
sticks and Oilers jerseys for Christmas, and the morning
before we left they headed off to the little inlet down the hill
from our cabin for one last game of shinny. After Mieka and
I had checked the cabin to make sure everything was
packed, we went down to the lake to watch. It was good to
stand breathing in the piny air and listening to the sounds of
skates slicing the ice and Angus's running commentary on
the game:

"A perfect pass from Harris to Angus Kilbourn — right to
his stick, deked the defenceman. Peter Kilbourn's not
looking happy. It's back to Harris. He's shooting for the
corner. It's a blistering slapshot but it's not enough – Angus
Kilbourn's in there . . ."

Mieka turned to me. She was wearing a new Arctic parka
Greg had given her for Christmas, and her cheeks were pink
with cold. My daughter had always despaired of her looks,
but that morning she was beautiful.

"Mum," she said, "let's take one last walk on the lake.
These guys are their own best audience."

We walked onto the ice, past the wood huts of the ice
fishers, toward the centre of the lake. It was a long walk
and when we finally turned and looked back toward the inlet
where the boys were skating, their orange and blue jerseys

were just scraps of colour in the grey sweep of land and lake and sky. They seemed so far away and vulnerable that I shivered and pulled my jacket tight around me.

"Cold?" Mieka asked.

"No, it's just . . . I don't know . . . usually the sun's out and the sky's blue and everything's like a postcard, but when it's grey like this, the lake scares me."

Mieka widened her eyes in exasperation. "The ice is about three feet thick here. We're perfectly safe."

"It's not that. It's just . . ." I smiled at her. "You're lucky you're sensible like your dad. Good gene selection. Come on, let's change the subject. It was a great holiday, wasn't it? And, Miek, I really enjoy Greg. He fits in so well."

Mieka smiled and looked toward the far shore. We were silent for a while, then she turned to me and took a deep breath. "Mum, I'm glad you like him. That makes my news a little easier."

Pregnant, I thought, looking at her bright, secret eyes. My mind raced – a wedding, of course. But why 'of course'? Women didn't bolt to the altar any more, but still, a baby. A new life . . .

"I'm quitting school to set up a catering business with Greg," she said.

"What?" I asked stupidly.

"A catering business. They're renovating the Old Court House, and there's a great space on the main floor – central, very posh, perfect location for what we're planning. Here's our idea – we're going to specialize in catering for businesses. We come to your offices or your boardroom and when you break for lunch or supper we serve you a really fine meal. No waiting. No wasting time. Everything fresh – supplies will be key. We'll pay for the best. Everything freshly prepared – we'll do the *mise en place* in the main kitchen and bring everything with us. Then when you're having a glass of wine –

good wine, we'll have a nice wine list – we'll cook for you, everything *à la minute*, and everything served by people who care about food. The place I'm after is the old small claims court – I'm going to call the place Judgements."

"No, you're not," I said harshly. "You're not calling it anything. You're going back to university next week."

She looked at me levelly. "Thanks for hearing me out."

"Mieka," I said, "I'm sorry. It was a shock – even the French – you got forty-three in French last semester. Where did all this fluency come from?"

She bit her lip and looked across the lake.

I started again. "Opening a catering business isn't something ordinary people do. It's something you talk about doing, like writing a novel or living on a Greek island. The food business is brutal, Miek. There was an article in the *Globe and Mail* last week that said for every two restaurants that open, three close."

She took a breath and turned to me. Her voice was controlled and it was determined. "Mum, I'm not opening a restaurant. Now come on. I have our business plan at the cabin: feasibility study, marketing surveys, projected financial statements – the works. We figure we can open the doors on Judgements for a hundred thousand dollars."

"Mieka – a hundred thousand! You've got to be crazy. Where are you going to get that kind of money?"

"Some of it we'll get from a bank – the way everybody else does. They're not keen about financing upscale catering businesses. The bank people I've talked to say they're too risky – capital intensive, labour intensive – you're right about that. But Judgements is going to work. Greg's uncle is going to arrange for a line of credit and Greg has a twenty-five-thousand-dollar inheritance from his grandfather that we're going to use." She took a deep breath. "Now, I guess you know what I'm going to ask you for . . ."

"Your money for university," I said.

"The money you and Dad put away for my future," she corrected gently.

"I'm not going to give it to you. Mieka, you got a thirty-two in Economics last semester. How in the name of God do you expect to run a business?"

She looked at me hard. "Do you realize that's twice you've mentioned my grades in the last five minutes? But maybe you're right. Maybe there's a clue in those numbers. Maybe the fact that, except when you beat it into me, I've gotten terrible grades should tell us both something. I'm not a student, Mum. I don't like to learn from books. I like to do things with my hands. And you know what? I'm good at what I like to do. Be happy for me." She laughed. "Lend me money. Give me my money. Daddy had enough set aside to get me through grad school. I know that. Well, I don't want grad school, and they won't want me, but I do want a chance at my business."

"No," I said.

"And that's it?" she said in a small, tight voice.

"Damn it, Miek. What am I supposed to say when I see you walking away from any possibility of a decent future? What did Greg's mother say when he told her he was quitting university?"

"He's not quitting."

I could feel the anger rising in my throat. "Well, that's just great. The girl quits school to put the guy through school. Mieka, I've seen this movie a hundred times."

"No, Mum, you have not seen this movie a hundred times. I'm not working at a dumb job to put my husband through med school. I'm an equal partner in a business. Greg is finishing his admin degree so when the time comes we'll know how to expand our business. We've made some good decisions here. Now you make a good decision. Face the fact that I'm just not university material."

I touched the sleeve of her jacket. "Mieka, please, you're not stupid."

She pulled up the hood of her parka and knotted it carefully under her chin. Suddenly her profile was alien. I didn't know her any more. When she spoke, her voice was patient and remote.

"Mum, I never thought I was stupid. I was just never good at school." She turned toward me and shrugged. "I was just never you."

For a few moments we stood there. Finally, wordless, we walked toward the cabin. For the first time in our lives, my daughter and I didn't seem to have much to say to each other.

When we got back, the boys were sitting at the kitchen table drying the blades of their skates, and the cabin had the cheerless feeling of a place that was about to be abandoned. It didn't take the kids long to pick up on the tension between Mieka and me. Even Angus didn't put up a fight when we started toward the cars. We all knew the holiday was over.

When Greg and Mieka's Audi got to the top of the hill, I waved. Greg turned and waved back but Mieka stared straight ahead, and in a moment the car disappeared and she was gone.

Beside me, Peter said, "I'll drive the first hour. Angus can bag out in the back seat. He was up half the night with that stupid game he bought himself for Christmas."

Peter and Mieka had always been close, and I could tell by the set of his jaw how upset he was.

"You're a good guy, Pete," I said.

He looked at me wearily. "Mieka's a good guy, too, Mum. Hang on to that thought."

At the edge of the park we stopped for gas. There was a rack full of Saskatoon papers by the cash register. Councillor Hank Mewhort was on the front page under a headline that said, "Vigil at the Mendel." He was holding a candle and, in the darkness, the play of light and shadow on his face made him look like a slightly cracked cherub. I bought a paper.

The story wasn't encouraging. There had been vigils in front of the gallery every night since Christmas. There were the usual interviews with people talking about pornography and community values, but things seemed to be turning ugly. The night before someone had hung an effigy of Sally from a tree in front of the gallery, and the crowd had pulled the effigy down and burned it.

It was a disturbing image. I closed the paper and looked out the car window. When the pine trees gave way to the white fields and bare trees of the open prairie, my eyelids grew heavy.

The radio was on and a man with a gentle, sad voice was talking about the dangers of genetic engineering in poultry. "So many species endangered," he said, "a virus could wipe out one of these new super breeds or some genetic problem . . . important to keep some of the original breeds as a safe-guard . . . so vulnerable . . . the world's more dangerous now . . . could die so easily . . ."

And then a man was laughing and Stuart Lachlan was saying, "Of course, it would have been better if Sally died," and I awoke with a start to the sun hot in my face and Stuart Lachlan's voice on the radio.

". . . realized instinctively that didactic art is trivial art and that the burden of dogma will always crush the artist's spirit."

"What is this, Pete?" I asked.

"Some arts show. Hey, you must trust my highway driving more these days. You were asleep for almost two hours. That's Stuart Lachlan talking about some book he's written about Sally. He just about put me under, too."

"You would have been on the edge of your chair if Sally were a quarterback."

He grinned. "Yeah, right, Mum."

Outside, the sky was grey, heavy with snow. In the car, Stuart Lachlan's voice droned on, patient, professionally exact.

"What people don't understand is that as a maker of art, Sally's always been a loner. She claims to be uncomfortable with movements and schools and labels. She says, 'When I'm in the studio I'm just a painter,' yet for all her disclaimers Sally Love has always been on the cutting edge of change in the art world. How do we explain that?" he asked rhetorically.

Out of nowhere, a hawk swooped across the highway and picked up a small animal from the ditch beside the road. It was a heart-stoppingly clean movement.

"Gotcha," I said.

"The explanation is simple," Stu said. "As a painter, Sally Love has always been self-conscious in the best sense of the word. She is acutely conscious of the people and places around her, and she has always managed to get herself into situations where she has been able to make significant art."

"And out of situations where she was unable to make significant art," the interviewer said flatly.

Stuart laughed, but his voice was tight. "Yes," he agreed, "and out of situations where she was unable to make significant art."

The interviewer thanked Stu; the music came up. I poured two cups of coffee from the Thermos and handed one to Peter.

"Peter," I said, "was I dreaming or did Stu say something about Sally dying?"

He looked at me quickly. "Yeah, it was at the beginning – something about the critic's art and how it's always better if the person you're writing about is dead. What he said was – now this isn't exact, but it's close – 'If they're dead, they

can't embarrass the writer by destroying all his theories.'
And then, Mum, he said something so shitty. He said, 'Of
course, as far as my critical appraisal of Sally's work is concerned it would have been better if Sally died.' I mean, isn't
that a little parasitic?"

"Parasites live off live tissues. It's saprophytes that eat
dead things." Angus's voice came loud and disoriented from
the back seat.

I turned to look at him. He was thirteen – not an easy age,
and there were times when he was not an easy kid.

"I see the reports of your death were greatly exaggerated,"
I said.

"What?" he asked, rubbing his eyes.

"You slept for over two hours. I'm glad to see you're
alive." I touched Peter on the hand. "We'd better put this
conversation on hold for a while. We can talk more about
Stuart and Sally when we get home."

But it was a long time before we did. Things happened.

Sally's Porsche was still in the driveway when we pulled up
at our house late in the afternoon. She came out to help us
carry in our luggage, and when it was all inside, she sat down
at the kitchen table. She didn't seem in a hurry to leave.

I went over and gave her a hug. "Make yourself comfortable," I said. "I've got some unfinished family business to
take care of. It won't take long."

She smiled. "I'm not going anywhere."

I picked up the kitchen phone and dialled Mieka's
number. Greg answered. When I asked for my daughter, he
sounded the same as he always did, laconic but pleasant. At
least he wasn't mad at me.

"Sorry, Jo. Mieka's in the tub, soaking."

"Safe from mothers who rail at her about her life," I said.

"For the time being, I guess she is," he said gently.

"Greg, I'm sorry. I shouldn't be involving you. It's between Mieka and me. It's just I love her so much and I worry. Have her call me, would you?"

"I'll do my best."

"Thanks," I said. "Damn it, why isn't anything ever simple?"

He laughed. "Well, you know what Woody Allen says. 'Life is full of anxiety, trouble and misery, and it's over too soon.' I'll have her call you, Jo."

I hung up and sat down opposite Sally at the kitchen table. Through the sliding doors to the deck, I could see the back-yard. A pair of juncos were fighting at the bird feeder.

"Everything okay now?" Sally asked.

"Mieka's boyfriend gave me a Woody Allen line. 'Life is full of anxiety, trouble and misery, and it's over too soon.'"

Sally looked thoughtful. "I'll drink to that," she said.

"You know," I said, "I think I will, too. What'll we have?"

"Bourbon," she said, leaning back in her chair. "Bourbon's good when you're talking about life." She was wearing a hound's-tooth skirt and a cashmere sweater the colour of Devon cream. It matched the bag she had talked Hugh Rankin-Carter into parting with the night of the opening. Her hair was looped back in a gold barrette, and the last sunlight of the day fell full on her face. She looked relaxed and at peace.

I came back and set our drinks down on the table. Sally picked up hers.

"So what's up with Mieka?" she asked.

"She wants to quit school and open a catering business."

"Is she any good?"

"As a cook? Terrific! And she's always been a good manager. It's just that her quitting school scares me."

"Does it scare her?"

"Not a bit, but still . . ."

"There is no 'but still.' Mieka's what? Twenty? Let her alone. Nobody likes a control freak. Think where I'd he if I'd let Nina choose a life for me." She winced. "No, don't think where I'd be. But look at me. A daughter any mother would be proud to tell her friends about. Now come on, let go. Let Mieka be Mieka. Let's drink to that and let's drink to the new year."

I smiled and lifted my glass. "To Mieka and to letting go. Happy New Year, Sally. I can tell just by looking at you, it's going to be wonderful. You look terrific."

"That's because, despite Councillor Mewhort and his campfires in front of the Mendel, things are working out. Stu's relented about Taylor. She's coming to live with me after her school has its midwinter break in February. I've called a friend in Vancouver to start looking around for a place for us – on the ocean and near a good school. Meanwhile Taylor and I are going to spend some time getting to know each other. Nina's idea. She says we really haven't spent much time together – which is true – and she says there's still too much ugliness about the Erotobiography to have Taylor move in with me, which is also true. There were a couple more incidents when you were away."

"Clea Poole?"

"Among others. A lot of people wrote to me. Half of them wanted me to make the city a better place by leaving, and the other half just wanted me to make them. My studio got broken into twice; someone put sugar in my gas tank, and I got some more Christmas presents."

"Oh, Sally, no."

"Nothing I couldn't handle, and the important thing is I'm getting Taylor."

I took another sip of my drink. "That really surprises me. I thought Stu would haul you into the tall grass over that one. What did you do? Sell your soul to the devil?"

Sally finished her drink and gave me an odd little smile. "No, to a mouse. I sold my soul to a mouse. Look, Jo, you must have a million things to do. I'd better get out of here. Thanks for the drink and for giving me a week in a real bed."

"Want to prolong the pleasures of the season and come for dinner tomorrow night? It's steak au poivre."

She slid her bag over her shoulder and stood up. "One of my favourites, but I think I'll pass this time. I'm going to spend the first day of the new year at the studio working. Even the crazies will have plans for tomorrow, so I might actually get something done."

I walked her to her car. She reached into the glove compartment and pulled out a package the size of a book. It was wrapped in brown paper, and for a minute I thought it must be a gift for the use of the house.

She handed it to me. "Jo, put this somewhere safe, would you? I don't seem to have any safe places any more. Just stick it up high where Angus won't get curious about it. And don't you get curious about it, either."

I raised my eyebrows. "What is it? A bomb?"

"No, nothing like that." Suddenly she grinned. "It's my insurance policy. If you lose it, I'm dead."

When I went in the house, the phone was ringing. It was Mieka, sounding friendly enough. She and Greg were spending New Year's Eve with friends but they'd be over, as planned, for dinner with us New Year's Day. She didn't say she had reconsidered her decision about school. She didn't say she realized I was right. She didn't say she was counting her blessings that I was her mother. All the same, she was coming to dinner. It was a start.

I spent the last night of the old year doing laundry and listening to the radio. Peter had picked up the dogs at the kennel, delivered them to our house, then gone off to a black-tie dinner at the Bessborough Hotel, so it was just

Angus and me. We had pancakes for supper, then he disappeared into the den and started calling all his friends, com-
paring holidays, getting caught up on what he'd missed.

About ten, I put the last load into the washing machine
and went upstairs to check on Angus. The television was
blaring. Dick Clark was standing in front of a room full of
people in party clothes and paper hats sweating under the
TV lights and trying to look as if they were having the time
of their lives. Angus was curled up on the couch, sleeping
the sleep of the just. I turned down the television, covered
him with an afghan and went into the kitchen to make a
pot of tea.

New Year's Eve at mid-life.

I let out the dogs for a final run and sat down at the
kitchen table. It was a magic night. The sky was bright with
stars, and the moonlight made the snow glitter. A party
night. Even the dogs seemed to be in a giddy mood; they
chased each other through the snow like puppies.

I thought of how happy my kids were, or at least how happy
they would be if I let them, and I thought about how well
the biography I was writing was going. With luck, by next
New Year's Eve it would be in the bookstores and I'd be safe
in a tenure-track position in some nice but not too demanding university. And I thought of Sally sitting in the chair
across from me that afternoon telling me how she and Stu
and Nina had reconciled their differences over Taylor. It
seemed as if everyone was, as we used to say in the sixties,
in a good space.

"All in all, not a bad year. Maybe the worst is over," I said
as I opened the back door to call the dogs in.

They wouldn't come. The backyard was deep, and the
dogs were at the farthest corner, at the gate that opened on
the back alley. They were barking at something. Going
crazy. Kids, I thought, out late for New Year's Eve.

"Sadie, Rose." I called the dogs' names in the voice that let them know I meant business. "Come on, get in here." They wouldn't come. There were stairs leading from the deck to the garden. I went halfway down and called again. Next door there was a party. A woman screamed, then laughed. I went the rest of the way down the stairs and started walking along the path to the gate. I was wearing runners, not great for walking in deep snow, and my feet were getting wet and cold.

"Damn," I said, "get in here. I've had enough." My voice sounded thin and vulnerable, but the dogs didn't take pity on me. They just stood there barking.

The woman at the gate didn't make any attempt to leave when she saw me. She was rooted in the snow with her video camera pointed at me, recording me as I walked toward her. I could see her face clearly in the light from my neighbour's garage. I could also see that she was wearing only a light jacket – not enough for December thirty-first in Saskatchewan. Suddenly, I was bone-tired.

"Clea," I said. "It's New Year's Eve. Time to wipe the slate clean and look ahead. Why don't you go home and get a good night's sleep. Everything will look better tomorrow."

"I'm not finished," she said dully.

"Not finished what?" I asked.

"Filming the history of womanswork," she said. "It should be recorded. All of it. Where it began. The women who helped." She waved a finger as if to chastise me. "The woman who didn't help. The record should be set straight. The gallery was a significant experiment. It deserves a memorial."

Seeing me talking to Clea apparently made her seem less of a threat to the dogs. They left us and went to the back door and waited. Without them, I wasn't so brave.

"Clea," I said, "if you need a cab, I'll go and call one for you. Otherwise, I'll just say good night. It's been a long day, and I'm tired."

She didn't say a word, just turned and walked down the alley.

I was shivering with cold and fear when I got in the house. I went straight to the kitchen. The package Sally had given me, her insurance policy, was still sitting on the kitchen table. I took it downstairs to the laundry room and hid it up high in a basket the kids had given me a hundred years ago for my sewing. No one, including me, ever went near it. I pulled my warmest sweats out of the dryer, walked down the hall to the bathroom and took a hot shower.

When I went upstairs to the kitchen, the tea in the pot was cold, but the Jack Daniel's bottle was still on the counter. I dumped the tea, made myself a bourbon and water, went down to the den and sat beside my sleeping son.

Five minutes to midnight in New York City. It was raining in Times Square, but nobody seemed to care. Slickers soaked, hair pasted against their faces by the rain, the tourists mugged for the TV cameras. At the bottom of the screen, the digital clock moved inexorably toward the new year. I took a deep pull on my drink and moved closer to Angus. The electronic apple in Times Square had started to fall – in the east, there were just seconds till midnight.

"Five, four, three, two, one," the crowd in New York chanted. Beside me, my son stirred in his sleep. "Happy New Year," screamed the people in Times Square. And in the room with me, the phone was ringing. I leaned across Angus to pick up the receiver.

"Happy New Year," I said.

"Not yet," said the voice on the other end. "There's still an hour left."

"Clea, please, leave it alone. Leave me alone."

There was silence on the other end of the phone.

"All right," I said, "if you've got nothing to say, I'm hanging up. I'm too old for pranks."

"This isn't a prank. This is my life." Her husky voice cracked with emotion. "This is my life. I need to talk to somebody about what to do next."

"I barely know you."

"But you know Sally."

For Clea Poole apparently that was recommendation enough. I closed my eyes and remembered Clea as she had been the night of Sally's opening: delicate, carefully groomed, buoyant about the work she was showing at the gallery.

"All right, Clea," I said wearily. "But not tonight."

"Tomorrow, then. Here at the Mendel. I'm working in the education gallery on an installation. I'm going to work through the night. I don't want to go back to my house. Holidays aren't good times when you're alone."

"No," I agreed, "they're not."

"I'll tell the security man to let you in," she said, and the line went dead.

On television, Dick Clark was saying, "Remember if you're driving tonight, make that one for the road a coffee." I turned off the TV, went upstairs and poured myself another Jack Daniel's. I wasn't driving anywhere.

The next morning as I walked across the bridge to the gallery I was tired and on edge. Peter had come home very late – not too late for an eighteen-year-old on New Year's Eve, but too late for a mother who can't fall asleep till she knows her kids are safe. And I wasn't looking forward to spending the first morning of the new year with Clea Poole.

The banners for Sally's show were still up at the gallery. A solitary picket was out front. The others had drifted away during the holidays, but this one was vigilant. Sally called him the Righteous Protester, and every day he had a new sign. Today's said, "Whatsoever a Man Soweth That Shall He Also Reap."

I waved to him as I ran up the steps to the gallery, but he didn't wave back. I waited five minutes in the cold before anyone came in answer to the security buzzer. The guard who finally opened the door was young enough to be my son. On the breast pocket of his uniform, his name was embroidered: Kyle. He seemed surprised to see me. Clea Poole, he said, had not left a message that I was to be admitted; if I insisted on coming in and looking for her, he would have to accompany me.

As we walked down the cool, quiet corridor toward the education gallery, I was furious. In all likelihood, Clea was safe at home in bed. To make matters worse, Kyle was dogging me in a way that suggested that if he left me alone, I would do unspeakable damage.

Outside the education gallery, he suddenly became human. As he pulled open the door, he grinned and made a sweeping gesture of presentation.

"Here we are. Hang on to your hat."

The room we were in was large and, except for one corner, dimly lit. In the area of full light, a naked woman lay on an operating table. Clea Poole was standing over her, drawing a scalpel carefully along the lower part of the woman's stomach. When Kyle called her name, Clea looked up.

"You can go," she said to Kyle. "Joanne is here to talk to me."

"Go ahead and look," Kyle said. "She won't bite."

The figure on the operating table seemed to be made of some sort of soft plastic. She was lifelike, but if she had had a life, it had been a hard one. She was covered with neatly stitched surgical incisions. There wasn't much of her that hadn't been cut open and sewn up: her eyelids, the hairline between her ear and her temple, her nose, her jawline, her breasts, the sides of her thighs.

"Good Lord," I said, "what's it supposed to be?"

"She's a scalpel junkie," Clea said. "An emblem of how society obsesses women with body image."

A half-moon line on the figure's lower stomach gaped open, and Clea removed a piece of foam and stuck it absent-mindedly in the back pocket of her jeans.

"She's part of a triptych," Clea said, although I hadn't asked. "It's an installation by an artist Izaak Levin is interested in. I'm just doing menial work, carrying out the artist's plans." She laughed. "No one better qualified than me for that. The junkie will be suspended from the ceiling. That," she said, pointing to a double bed in the corner, "will be brought over and put underneath her."

Half the bed was traditionally bridal, soft-looking, inviting, covered with a satiny white duvet. At the head of that part of the bed was a pillow embroidered "His." The other half of the bed was bare, just a frame covered with the kind of barbed wire used in electric fences to keep cattle confined. In the half light of the gallery, the wire hummed and sparked blue. The pillow on that side of the bed said "Hers."

"The camera will be moved over, too," Clea said, pointing to the ceiling where, unheeded, a video camera whirred. "They're going to tape people's reactions to the junkie. The third part of the concept is a coffin. They're delivering it at the end of the week."

Clea's voice was curiously detached, the voice of a person who'd lost interest in her own life. Across the room the red light of the emergency exit glowed invitingly.

"'Skin-deep,' that's the name of the installation," she said, walking back to the operating table. She picked up a darning needle and threaded it expertly with catgut. "They tell us all we're good for is being caretakers of our surfaces. We've lost all the ground we gained in the seventies, you know. We've been battered, ghettoized by the sexual hierarchy."

She began stitching the incision on the woman's stomach. She sewed mechanically and well, and as she sewed she talked listlessly about women and art and Sally.

"History is repeating itself," she said. "We have to reclaim our own terrain. It's important that she's with other women now. Not women like you. She's a catalyst. She used to know what the male power machine did to women. She knew we had to get past male critics and dealers and collectors and create a nonjudgemental environment where women could show their work. She was wearing a T-shirt the first time I saw her. She was the most beautiful creature I'd ever seen. The womanswork gallery was her idea. China painting, performance art, soft sculpture, murals, needlework, body art – we did it all. It was the best time of my life. The only time of my life. I thought it meant the same thing to her, but it didn't. 'Time to move along,' that's what she says. It's my life, but it's just a blip on the screen for her, like neo-expressionism or post mod. Time to move along. Time to let go." When she stopped sewing and looked at me, her eyes were filled with tears. "She knows I can't let go. Letting go is for people who know they won't fall."

"Clea, how can I help?" I asked. "What do you expect me to do?"

"What do I expect you to do?" she repeated. "I expect you to stop turning her against me. I've thought about this, Joanne. It's no coincidence that Sally decided to sell our gallery shortly after you came back on the scene. You're one of those women who's been co-opted by the system. You don't care about other women."

I tried to keep the anger out of my voice. "Clea," I said, "that is so untrue and so unfair. I've never tried to undermine your relationship with Sally."

She finished sewing the incision, knotted the thread and snipped the catgut with her scalpel.

"I don't believe you," she said flatly. "If I were you, I'd get out of here now, Joanne. You're making things worse. Cut your losses. Isn't that what people like you do when you're in a no-win situation?" The tears were streaming down her face, but she didn't seem to notice them. "Is loss-cutting a skill you're born with?" she asked, her voice thick with pain. "I need to know this, Joanne. Is it too late for me to learn how to cut my losses? Have I missed the deadline?"

I stepped toward her, but she raised her hand as if to ward off a blow.

There was nothing I could do. "Good-bye, Clea," I said. "Get some help. Please, for all our sakes, get some help."

At the door, I turned and looked. Clea was standing behind her operating table watching me with dead eyes. In her hand, the scalpel glinted lethal and bright.

It was good to step outside into the sunshine of an ordinary day. It was even a relief to see the Righteous Protester making his lonely rounds. Bizarre as he was, he at least seemed connected to a recognizable world.

As I stood looking at the deserted street in front of the gallery, I started to shake. The encounter with Clea had disturbed me more than I realized. I didn't make a conscious decision to cross Spadina Crescent and walk up the block to Stuart Lachlan's house. Reflexively, I did what I had done a thousand times when life overwhelmed me. I went to Nina.

She came to the door herself. As always, she was immaculate. Her dark hair was brushed into a smooth page boy, her makeup was fresh, and she was wearing a black knit skirt, a white silk blouse and an elegant cardigan, black with a pattern of stylized Siamese cats worked in white.

When she saw me, her face was radiant. "Oh, Jo, come in out of the cold and visit. This is the best surprise, especially because I have a surprise for you, too. Let me take your coat and then we'll go and see an old friend."

I followed her into the living room. "Now, look," she said. "How's this for bringing back the memories?"

In front of her was the drop-leaf desk she'd had in the sitting room of her Toronto house. She was right. It did bring back memories.

They weren't all pleasant. The desk was Chinese Chippendale, lacquered black with gilt trim. Nina used to keep a lacquerware water jar on it. Painted fish swam on that jar – perfect, serene in their ordered, watery world. When my mother was at her worst, I would come to Nina and she would tell me to sit at that desk and try to close out everything but the smooth passage of the bright fish as they swam around and around the jar. It always worked. That desk had been my refuge, and Nina had been my rock. None of my mother's dark hints about Nina's character or my blindness to her faults could erode that.

Behind me, Nina, her voice vibrant and affectionate, said, "We've weathered a lot of storms at this desk, haven't we, Jo? I'm leaving it to you in my will."

I felt a chill. I put my arm around her shoulders and breathed in the familiar fragrance of her perfume.

"Well, when you leave, I'm going, too. My world would be a desolate place without you."

She laughed. "Don't break out the crepe, yet. I'm not planning to leave the party for a long time."

We brought coffee and some still-warm banana bread into the living room and sat at a small table near the front window. There was a bouquet of white tulips on the table, and the sun bathed them in wintery light. This bright and civilized room seemed light-years removed from Clea Poole's dark and pain-filled world, but it was of Clea we talked as the good smells of coffee and fresh baking surrounded us and the crystal purity of one of the Brandenburg Concertos floated in from another room.

I told Nina everything, and as I talked I realized how much Clea had scared me. "She's in the middle of a terrible breakdown," I said, "and she's unreachable. I think all the things she does – phoning Sally fifty times a night, stalking us with her camera, working on that extraordinary exhibition – I think all those things seem logical to her, and what terrifies me is that I don't know what might seem logical to her next. I think she's reached the point where she's capable of anything. She's even made some oblique threats to me."

Nina frowned. "Jo, I'll give you the same advice someone should give Sally. Stay away from Clea Poole. Stuart's had some dealings with her in the past, and he thinks she could be violent. If she sees you as a rival, God knows what she'll do. Sally's used to dealing with people like that, but you're not. Be careful, Jo. Please, be careful."

"Nina's right," said a man's voice behind us. "I can attest to the fact that Clea Poole is a nasty enemy." I looked up and there was Stuart Lachlan. I wondered how long he'd been standing there. I had expected the prospect of Taylor's leaving to devastate him, but he looked fine. He was wearing a black and white pullover that was obviously the masculine version of the cardigan Nina was wearing, and as he bent to embrace me, I thought I smelled the kind of lemony fragrance she liked on him. She was having an influence.

He sat down beside her on the love seat and looked at me earnestly. "I'm serious, Jo. When Sally and I were first married, Clea did some amazing things."

"Sally told me about the hair incident."

He winced. "You know, then. Clea's been better for so long, I guess we all thought that breakdown was an isolated thing. In fact, I arranged for her to do that work on the installation at the gallery. Usually a student would do that, but Clea seemed desperate for diversion."

"Stu, I just came from the Mendel, and Clea didn't look diverted to me. She looked like somebody who shouldn't be spending her days and nights working with surgical instruments."

Nina shuddered. "I'm sure Stuart will look in first thing tomorrow, Jo. Now could we please talk about something pleasant? I don't think we've even said Happy New Year to one another."

I smiled. "Happy New Year – I hope it's a wonderful year for you both. You deserve it. Stu, that was such a generous arrangement about Taylor that you worked out with Sally. And, Nina, you deserve praise, too. I know how much being with Taylor day to day means to you. Not many people could have been so selfless."

They looked at one another quickly, then Nina reached across the table and patted my hand. "Jo, if it were anyone but you, we'd take the praise and run, but you deserve the truth. Sally will never take Taylor. Stuart and I feel the idea of being a mother and mentor is just a flirtation for her. She's between partners, and for Sally that always means a drop in creative energy. As soon as there's a new relationship, she'll be back painting fifteen hours a day, and she'll forget all about her daughter." Nina leaned forward and touched the petals of the flowers in front of her. "Mark my words, when the tulips bloom in the flower beds out front, Taylor will still be in this house."

In the background the Brandenburg soared. Stu and Nina sat side by side, quietly waiting for me to say something. I hadn't noticed until that moment how much they were alike physically: the same dark hair, the same fine features, the same intensity as they waited for reassurance.

I couldn't give it to them. "There's nothing in the world I wouldn't do for you, Nina. And, Stu, you know I want you to be happy, but I think you're wrong about this. Sally is very serious about having Taylor live with her. She told me last night she's been looking for a house in Vancouver – something near a good school for Taylor. As painful as it is, I think you have to be realistic. Sally plans to take her daughter with her in February."

They looked quickly at each other, but neither said anything. When I stood up to leave, they both followed me to the hall. It wasn't until Stuart was helping me on with my parka that he finally spoke.

"She may not have that chance, you know. Events sometimes intervene."

I kissed Nina on the cheek and grasped Stu's hand. "Don't count on it, Stu, just please don't count on it."

# CHAPTER

# 6

I slept for a couple of hours when I got home, and by the time I finished lunch, I felt ready to start the new year. I spent the afternoon curled up by the fireplace reading an exposé of our current prime minister by his ex-chef. When I was finished, I was glad I did my own cooking. Around four, Mieka and Greg arrived with the news that there was a blizzard on the way, and the RCMP were telling everybody to stay off the roads. By the time Peter brought Christy over, the snow had started, the wind had picked up, and I sent Angus down to wash another load of sheets in case everyone stayed the night.

Dinner was an easy, happy meal, and afterwards it was good to sit in the candlelight, finishing off the Beaujolais and watching the storm gathering power outside. Safe. We were safe at home. We had finished cleaning up and the kids had gone downstairs to watch the last of the Bowl games when the phone rang.

At first I didn't recognize the voice.

"Jo, I'm in trouble. Big trouble. I just got to the gallery and . . ."

I could hear sirens. They were so faint I couldn't tell, at first, if they were coming from the TV downstairs or the phone. The doubt didn't linger.

"Oh, God, the cops are here," she said. "I'm just going to stick where I am, Jo, at the Mendel. I already said that, didn't I? Jo, she's dead. Clea's dead."

"Do you have a lawyer, Sally? Someone I can call?" On the other end of the line there was silence and then a click as the receiver was replaced.

My parka and boots were by the kitchen door. I started down to the family room to tell the kids where I was going, then changed my mind. I didn't have time for explanations. I left a note on the table, picked up my car keys and headed for the garage. As I walked through the breezeway, I heard the crowd in Pasadena roar. It sounded like a touchdown.

When I pulled the Volvo out of the driveway, I leaned forward automatically to turn on the radio. Pete had left it tuned to a soft rock station, and a woman named Brie, who sounded too young to be out after dark, was saying her station was going to get us through the blizzard by playing the songs of summer. As I pulled onto Clarence Avenue, the snow had become a dense and dizzying vortex that looked capable of sucking me through the windshield, and Eddie Cochran was singing that there ain't no cure for the summertime blues.

There was also no visibility. I inched along using the streetlights as reference points until I came to the intersection of Clarence and College, just before the University Bridge. As I pulled onto the bridge, Brie said the Lovin' Spoonful were going to do their classic "Summer in the City"; a hundred feet beneath me was the South Saskatchewan River, killingly cold but frozen only in parts because of the runoff from the power station. To my right, the guardrails that kept me from plunging over the top were an incandescent fuzz, but I couldn't see in front of me – in fact, I didn't know where in front of me was. Suddenly, I became convinced that I'd drifted out of my lane. I turned off the radio and rolled down my window so I could hear any car that might be about to drive head-on into mine. I could hear the wind keening along the river, but there were no sounds of cars. "I'm the only car on the bridge," I said aloud. That should have made me feel better, but it didn't.

When I turned off the bridge onto Spadina Crescent I could see the Mendel's orange security lights. The word *security* had never seemed sweeter or more ironic. The front of the gallery was brightly lit. Sally's Porsche was there. So was a police car, and two more were just pulling up. I could see an officer sealing off the entrance to the gallery with tape. It didn't seem likely he was going to invite me in.

Frustrated, I rested my forehead against the steering wheel. I thought of Sally surrounded by police in that room with the scalpel junkie and the electric bed. And then I thought of the red glow of the exit sign over the emergency door in the education gallery. They might not have blocked that door off yet. It was certainly worth a shot. I drove past the gallery and parked on the side street north of the grounds. I covered my face with a scarf and started off across the lawn to the gallery. It was slow going. My legs ached from the effort of plodding through the heavy snow, but I held an image of Sally in my mind and kept trudging. Finally I could see the outline of the door to the education gallery, and I began to run toward it.

There was a little stand of bushes beside the door, and the snow had drifted deeply in front of it. When I climbed through the snowdrift, my foot caught on something and I fell face down in the snow. But not wholly in the snow. My legs were on top of something. When I reached my right arm out to see what it was, I touched the silky smoothness of a down-filled coat. It felt like the padding in a coffin. I moved my hand up, and under the snow my fingers touched the contours of a human face. When I sat up, I could see the orange glare of the security lights reflected in his eyes.

I had never seen him up close, but I would have known his face anywhere.

It was the Righteous Protester.

Suddenly I began to shake. I pushed myself up and ran toward the door. I pounded it, shouting for help, screaming for Sally. Desperate, I tried the knob. The door opened easily, and in a minute, I stepped from the cold into the hot craziness of a nightmare.

There was a smell in the room. Something familiar, the smell of meat cooking. It took my eyes a few moments to adjust themselves to the half light and then to take in the scene.

Clea had made real progress on the installation since morning. The scalpel junkie had had her last surgery and was suspended from the ceiling on wires, like a marionette. Beneath her was the bridal bed. There weren't any blue sparks coming off the wires. Someone had turned off the power. But there was a figure on the bed. Clea Poole was lying face down on the barbed wire. She was naked. When I saw her, I knew where the meat smell was coming from. The hooks from the barbed wire must have embedded themselves in her skin; until the power had been turned off, Clea had been slowly cooking. I closed my eyes. I didn't want to see any more. The room swayed around me. In a minute I felt an arm around my shoulders, and I heard a familiar voice, choked but recognizable.

"I knew you'd come," Sally said. Those were the only words she had time for. Suddenly we weren't alone any more. Two policemen had come over: a young man who looked the way Burt Reynolds must have looked when he was twenty, and a heavier man. They seemed to have just arrived; their cheeks were still pink with cold. They were both very young, and despite their uniforms and their heavy regulation winter boots, it soon became apparent that nothing in the police college had prepared them for this.

The Burt Reynolds officer looked up at the scalpel junkie and said in a tone of awe, "Jesus Christ, it must have been some sort of cult thing – a ritual murder or something." His partner didn't reply. He had taken one look at Clea and bent double with the dry heaves.

"There's another man outside in the snow," I said in a voice I didn't recognize.

The heavy cop straightened up, squared his shoulders and walked to the exit door. "I'll check it out," he said, and I thought how grateful he would be to fill his lungs with cold fresh air and have a chance to redeem himself.

The Burt Reynolds officer turned to us and said in carefully measured tones, "I think the inspector is going to be pretty interested in talking to you."

Sally watched him walk across the room.

"You know, I've never had a cop," she said.

"You'll have the whole Saskatoon force to choose from before this is over," I said, and I looked around that scene from hell and thought I had never said a stupider thing in my life.

In fairness, there didn't seem to be much to say. Sally and I lapsed into silence until Inspector Mary Ross McCourt came over and introduced herself. She didn't look like a cop. She was about average height, not good looking, but carefully groomed. Her hair was bleached an improbable white blond, and her makeup was dramatic, red 1940s lipstick, scarlet fingernails, but her eyes behind the bright blue eye shadow were intelligent and knowing. I had the sense, as my grandmother used to say, that not much got by her.

Inspector McCourt quickly established two things: in

response to my question, she said that, yes, she was the niece of my old friend Hilda. But it was clear from her manner that I was not to presume that friendship with her aunt put us on social terms.

The Burt Reynolds constable brought her a chair, but Mary Ross McCourt did not sit down. She stood with her hands resting on the chair back and looked at Sally and me. Psychological advantage to the inspector.

"Under normal circumstances," she said, "we'd go downtown, but those streets are lethal. It would be unconscionable to ask you to drive on them." She looked hard at Sally and me. "I'm sure you agree that there's been enough death for one night."

Sally and I exchanged glances: two schoolgirls in the principal's office struggling with the etiquette of whether to answer a rhetorical statement. We didn't say anything. But we didn't stay silent. I had a question of my own, and it wasn't rhetorical.

"How did she die?" I asked.

Mary Ross McCourt sighed. "The pathologist's initial judgement is a bullet through the heart. About here," she said, tapping the centre of her own chest with a scarlet-tipped finger. "Now, Ms. Love, I wonder if you'd be kind enough to move out of earshot while I talk to Mrs. Kilbourn."

Sally picked up her chair and carried it over to the area behind the scalpel junkie. Inspector McCourt moved her chair a little closer to mine but she still didn't sit down. Up close, her hair was as blond and fluffy as Barbie's, but she didn't sound like a Barbie.

"Mrs. Kilbourn," she said, "I want you to tell me about your life in the last few hours. Don't edit. Everything is significant."

I couldn't seem to stop talking – shock, I guess, or aftershock. Mary Ross McCourt listened impassively, like a psychoanalyst in the movies. All the while I rattled on about preparing and eating the dinner with my children and driving through the blizzard, the crime site experts moved purposefully around us dusting surfaces for fingerprints; taking photographs; putting evidence in what looked like heavy plastic freezer bags; drawing floor plans. Across the room, prim as a schoolgirl, Sally sat in the shadow of the scalpel junkie. The scene was as surreal as a Salvador Dali landscape.

When I finished, the inspector thanked me and suggested I stay in touch with the police. Then her professionalism broke. She took a step closer to me. Suddenly the eyes behind the bright blue shadow were glacial, and her voice was low with fury.

"This is a terrible, terrible crime," she said. "Whoever did this will never know another peaceful moment this side of the grave." For the first time that night, Mary Ross McCourt reminded me of her aunt.

The inspector took her chair over to where Sally was sitting, and I was interested to see that she established the same relationship with Sally as she had had with me: questioner standing, witness sitting. Then they brought in the Righteous Protester and some new cops came to take Clea's body and I lost interest in police procedures.

I followed along as they carried the bodies toward the front door. At first, the scene outside seemed like an instant replay of the night Erotobiography opened. The blizzard had stopped, and some hardy souls had braved the snow to come and gawk. The media people were there, too, adjusting equipment, waiting. But there were differences. This time the centre of attention wasn't Sally Love; it was the two blanket-covered shapes on the stretchers being loaded into twin ambulances. And this time the target of the crowd's moral outrage wasn't art but murder.

I was standing in the foyer, watching the ambulances pull

away, when Sally came up beside me. She couldn't have been with Mary Ross McCourt ten minutes.

I was surprised. "You certainly got off lightly," I said.

Sally shrugged. "I didn't have much to say. Jo, I haven't got an alibi. I was working all day in the studio. I didn't go out. I didn't see anybody until I ran into one of the merry pranksters in my driveway after Clea called. He was hunkered down behind the Porsche – probably giving me a flat tire."

"In the middle of a blizzard?" I asked.

"Jo, these guys are on a holy mission. Snow doesn't mean diddly to them."

"I hope you told Inspector McCourt," I said. "Sal, that could be important. Did you notice anything about him that could help the police find him?"

"Sure," she said, "he hates art, he hates me, and he was wearing a ski mask. That should narrow it down for them. But I got my revenge. I stole his tuque."

"What did Inspector McCourt say?" I asked.

"About the hat?"

"No, about the whole thing?"

Sally shrugged. "What could she say? She did her best Katharine Hepburn imitation of the public official who means business, then she just gave up – probably told me what she told you: 'Don't leave town. Keep in touch.' Now come on. Let's get out of here. My bravado is failing fast."

"We still have the rest of that bottle of Jack Daniel's at my house," I said. "Bourbon's good for bravado – actually I could use a little bravado myself. Let's go."

My kids greeted us at the door, white-faced and concerned. The local TV station had interrupted the Rose Bowl festivities to show the bodies of Clea Poole and the Righteous Protester being loaded into ambulances, and there had been a shot of Sally and me running for her car. Pete helped us off with our coats, and Greg, without being asked, brought us each a stiff drink. I was liking him better by the moment. I gave the kids an abbreviated account of what we knew, assured them that we were okay and told them they could get back to what they had been doing. Sally and I needed to talk.

We took our drinks downstairs to the family room. There was a fire, and Sally sprawled on a rocker near the fireplace. I curled up on the couch in front of it.

"I can't get warm," Sally said.

"Here," I said, handing her an afghan. "Mieka made this for me the year she broke her leg skiing."

Sally wrapped it around her shoulders. "I wonder if Taylor will ever want to make an afghan for her notorious mother."

"Sure," I said. "Notorious mothers are the best kind."

Sally smiled and lifted her glass. "To mothers," she said. Then her smile faded. "And to Clea Poole, may she rest in peace."

We drank, and Sally said thoughtfully, "You know, Jo, I'm glad she's dead. She was my – what was that bird the old sailor had hung around his neck in the poem?"

"An albatross," I said.

"Right. Clea was my albatross. She wanted me to carry her around forever. She would have done anything for me; you know, she did some terrible things. She had no morality when it came to me."

Instinctively, I looked over my shoulder to see if anyone had heard her. "Sally, you can say that to me, but I'd be careful not to say it to anyone else. Clea didn't put a bullet through her own heart and throw herself down on that bed because she was in a snit. Somebody murdered her, and until the police find out who did, you're going to have to watch what you say."

The fire was dying down, and I got up and put on another log. Behind me, Sally said, "I wonder who they think killed her? The nakedness makes it look like some kind of sex thing."

I shuddered. "You mean fun and games that got out of hand?" I asked. "Is that a possibility? You've known her all these years. Were there other connections, another relationship that might have gone sour?"

"All her relationships turned sour," Sally said flatly. "This city is filled with her failed relationships. Those baby cops we saw tonight are going to learn a lot about life before they're through with Clea." She stood up and stretched her arms above her head. "I've got to make tracks, Jo. That car of mine is fairly noticeable, and it's only a matter of time before the media people start beating down your door."

"Sal, stay here. The roads are terrible. I can open out this couch for you."

"No," Sally said. "The best thing for me right now is work. Take my mind off things. I'm going to go to the studio, take a bath, crack open my Christmas Courvoisier and make some art."

I walked her upstairs and stood in the entrance hall as she put on her boots and parka. At the door, she turned and hugged me.

"Thanks for everything. I'm not sure I could have made it if you hadn't been there." She smiled. "People can always count on Jo, can't they?" she said, and then she walked down our front path and vanished into the night.

I woke up early the next morning, anxious and restless. When I went down to make coffee, the sky was beginning to lighten, and I looked out on a white world. New snow was everywhere. The tracks I had made New Year's Eve when I'd gone to the bottom of the garden and found Clea waiting were gone. Clea's tracks would be gone, too – all her tracks, everywhere, filled in with snow as if she had never been.

I went out and picked up the morning paper from my
mailbox. The double homicide had beaten out the blizzard in
the headlines. Pictures of Clea and the Righteous Protester
were on the front page. She was graduating from university,
and he was standing in front of the Mendel with his placard
and his Bible. I threw the paper unread on the breakfast table,
went upstairs, showered and dressed. I still felt lousy, so I
came downstairs, picked up the keys to the Volvo and headed
out, figuring that maybe a drive would help.

Inevitably, I guess, I was drawn to the gallery. In the first
light of morning, it looked quite festive. The bright yellow
of the banners with Sally's name was matched by the bright
yellow crime scene tape; there were police around the front
entrance, and on the lawn, police dogs were pawing at the
snow. Other people had decided to take in the murder
scene, too, and traffic was slow. I was inching along when I
looked across the road and saw Stuart Lachlan out on his
front lawn. His house was close enough that I had a clear
view of what he was doing. Bundled against the cold, he was
repairing one of Taylor's snow people. Someone had knocked
off an arm and caved in its side. Stu was methodically
repairing the damage. In the doorway, I could see Nina's
neat figure, watching.

I drove past the gallery and made a U turn. I pulled over
to the curb in front of number seventeen and rolled down my
window. Stuart came over immediately and leaned in. When
she saw me, Nina ran out, too, and stood shivering behind
him. She was immaculate as always but she looked tired and
old, and I realized what a toll all this was taking on her.

"I guess there's no point asking if you heard about Clea,"
I said. "I couldn't sleep, either. But I didn't think of making
a snowman as therapy."

Stu looked at me gravely. "It's not therapy, Jo. It was van-
dalism. I didn't want Taylor to wake up and see her snow

lady wrecked. Nina was out here trying to repair it first, but
. . . there are things a man has to do."

I looked to see if he was joking. He wasn't. "You're a good
father, Stu," I said, and meant it. "Anyway, I'm glad to see
you're up and about. You're both okay, aren't you?"

Stu shook his head and laughed humourlessly. "Couldn't
be better. Have you read your morning paper? The media
are making certain connections between the murders and
Erotobiography. Of course, Sally's being discovered at the
scene of the crime didn't help matters. On the radio this
morning there was a not exactly veiled suggestion that if I
hadn't been so anxious to push my wife's pornography, two
more people would be greeting the dawn today. And the
gallery's a disaster – police everywhere. Tracking dogs
sniffing the galleries. Doors left open. Temperature control
all shot to hell. I was over there this morning pleading with
the police to let me move some paintings into the vault
until they're through." He raked his hand through his thin-
ning hair. "If I'd known there was going to be such chaos, I
wouldn't have . . . ."

"You wouldn't have what, Stuart?" Nina's voice sounded
small and frightened.

He gave her an odd look. "I wouldn't have been so eager
to accept Sally's offer to donate Erotobiography to the
Mendel. What did you think I was going to say, Nina?"
There was an ugly edge to his voice. The spoor of murder
and suspicion was already changing everything.

"I don't know," she said vaguely, "something else." And
then she asked the painful question, the one we'd all backed
away from.

"Who do they think did it, Joanne? Is Sally a suspect?"

"I don't think they've gotten that far yet," I said. "Listen,
I didn't tell you, but I was there at the gallery last night. I . . .
I was the one who found the Righteous Protester."

I could hear Nina's intake of breath. She looked quickly at Stu. In the hypercharged atmosphere of that morning, I could see the fear in her eyes.

"I know," I said. "It's terrifying, all of it, but, Nina, they'll find out who really committed the murders. The police inspector who interviewed us last night looked as if she could see through walls. When she gets this case put together, she'll know Sally was just in the wrong place at the wrong time."

"Thank God," said Stu.

"Yes," I agreed. "Thank God. Stu, you'd better get Nina back inside. It's too cold to be out with just a sweater. I'll talk to you later. Ni, don't worry. Everything's going to be all right. It really is."

As I turned onto the University Bridge, I wondered if my assurances had sounded as hollow to Nina's ears as they had to mine. I looked back at Stuart Lachlan's house. Stu and Nina were standing on the front lawn watching me, and Taylor had come out and joined them. Behind them, in exactly the same grouping – Daddy on the left, Mummy on the right and the little girl safe between them – was Taylor's family of snow people. As Angus would say, "Deadly."

I drove straight to my office at the university and worked for a couple of hours. I made up a syllabus for each of my classes, checked some handouts and read over my lecture notes for the first day – busywork to make me believe I was in charge of my world.

It was a little after noon when I went home to the hollow feeling of an empty house. There was an empty ice-cream pail on the counter in the kitchen, and when I put it under the sink to keep kitchen scraps in, I noticed two burrito wrappings in the garbage. Wherever they were, Peter and Angus were well fed.

I found their note on the kitchen table. They'd gone tobog-ganing at Cranberry Flats with some of Peter's friends from the university. They'd be home for supper. I could imagine how pleased Pete would be to have Angus along. I made myself a sandwich, then I peeled a bag of onions and threw them in the processor to slice for onion soup. Homemade soup would taste pretty good after an afternoon tobogganing.

I was just cleaning up when the phone rang. It was Sally. Her gun was missing.

"What gun?" I said. "For God's sake, what kind of person owns a gun?"

"A person like me who works alone at night in a house that sometimes has a couple of hundred thousand dollars' worth of art lying around. God damn it, Jo, don't yell at me. Stu bought the gun for me the first year we were married, and it was a good idea. That studio of mine is right on the river bank. Anyone could break in. And someone has. Remember I told you I had two break-ins over Christmas? Well, both times whoever was there left things behind: more used sanitary napkins, a bag of kitty litter, also used, and some stuff that's too disgusting to talk about. But the point is, because they were leaving things, I never checked to see if things were missing. The paintings were okay, and that's about all that's of interest there."

"Except your gun," I said.

"Yes, except my gun," she repeated. "And according to the police, it appears to have been the same kind as the one that did the job on Clea and poor old Righteous Protester."

"How do they know?"

"The same way they knew to look for a gun at my house in the first place. From the registration. God, Jo, it looks like I've really managed to get myself up shit creek."

The realization seemed to hit us both at the same time, but I was the one who put it into words.

"Sally, I think we're going to have to stop talking about what you've managed to do to yourself. Too many things are going wrong for you. The police show up at the gallery as soon as you discover Clea's body; your gun, apparently the same kind as the one that committed the murders, suddenly disappears. I think there's somebody else involved here."

Her voice on the other end of the line was small and sad. "Yeah, I think you're right, Jo. And you know what else? I think whoever wants me up shit creek is doing everything they can to make sure I don't have a paddle."

# CHAPTER

# 7

When I read the paper's lead story the morning of Clea's funeral I could feel my throat closing. The police had started to give the media details about their investigation, and there weren't many arrows pointing away from Sally and me. There was one item of hard news: Kyle, the museum guard, told the police that minutes before they arrived, the burglar alarm had gone off in the delivery area at the back of the gallery. When he went out to investigate, he saw a figure running down the hill toward the river bank. The snow was so heavy that he couldn't give the police a description, couldn't in fact tell for certain whether the runner had been male or female. Kyle had given chase but when he heard the siren from the police car, he returned to the gallery. The only thing that seemed to be missing from the gallery was the film from the video camera suspended over the bridal bed.

A mystery runner and an empty camera: it wasn't much.

The human interest angle was more fertile ground. From the beginning, the local paper couldn't seem to get enough of Clea and Sally. The morning after the murder, the obituary column had carried the details of Clea's funeral: services were to be conducted at the University Women's Centre by a woman named Vivian Ludlow from the radical feminist community. She taught a course called Human Justice, and I knew her slightly from the university. Interment was at a cemetery on the east side of the city. While men were welcome at the interment, they would not be permitted to attend the funeral service.

The paper managed to repeat the details of the funeral arrangements in most of the stories about Clea's life and death. Those few lines always gave a titillating but not libellous spin to their stories. Clea's association with Sally at womanswork; the arson that destroyed their gallery; the public outcry against the bisexual imagery of Erotobiography: all were suddenly set against a dark feminist world, a world where men were not welcome. It was hot stuff.

The Righteous Protester wasn't hot stuff. Even on the day of his funeral, he only rated a column and a half on page three. His name was Reg Helms, and as I read his obituary, I was struck again with how sad and stunted his life had been: a childless marriage to a woman who had died the year before of cancer, no friends to speak of, and a dead-end clerical job with a company called Peter's Pumpkin Seeds. Reg Helms was a great writer of letters to the newspaper; and every talk-show host in town recognized his voice. His preoccupation was our disintegrating society, and it was a theme he played with variations. Sometimes it was Quebec that was destroying the country, sometimes ethnic groups or Aboriginal peoples, but the subject that really warmed his heart was sexual permissiveness. Sally's show had been a holy mission for him. He had been fifty-four years old when he died.

The facts of Reg Helms's life had become as familiar to me as my own, but today there was something different. There was a final paragraph that laid out the medical details of his death. Helms had died of a bullet in the carotid artery.

The pathologist said death had come swiftly; nonetheless, there had been a second shot. Police theorized that when Reg Helms had raised his hand to his shattered throat, his murderer had fired again. The second bullet had struck Helms's watch. He had died at 6:21 on Tuesday, January first. His watch had recorded hour, minute, day and date. Cosmic timekeeping.

As soon as I saw the numbers, I felt a rush of excitement. Sally's phone call had come at ten to seven, and she had told me she'd just arrived at the gallery. I'd left home immediately. Under ordinary circumstances, I could have been at the gallery in ten minutes, but the blizzard and the walk across the lawn outside the gallery had slowed me. It would have been after seven when I found Reg Helms's body. At 6:21 I'd been at home with my kids cleaning up after dinner, getting ready to watch the end of the Rose Bowl game. I had an alibi. And if there was justice, Sally would have one, too.

She answered the phone on the first ring. When I told her about the story in the paper, she was restrained.

"It's great for you, Jo. Really, I'm happy and relieved that you're off the hook. It was awful knowing I'd involved you in all this. But it's no out for me. I don't know what time I got to the gallery. I don't even wear a watch. If you say I called you at ten to seven, then I must have gotten to the Mendel at about a quarter to. I called you as soon as I saw Clea."

"But, Sal, don't you see, I can tell the police that. I can swear to it."

"It's not enough. My best friend swearing that I told her I'd just arrived at the scene of a crime and found a body – it's just too thin, Jo. The cops would blow that alibi out of the water in about eleven seconds. I need more than that. I've been sitting here figuring out times. Let's say I got to the Mendel at 6:45. The roads were bad so it took me about ten minutes to drive there. That puts me out in front of my house at 6:35. And I must have been out there five minutes or so having my altercation with the guy in the ski mask." She laughed. "That probably happened around 6:30, so he'd be the one to give me the alibi. Do you think I can count on him?"

"Stranger things have happened," I said.

"No," Sally said, "stranger things than that have not happened. Face it, Jo. Nothing's changed. I'm still up the creek."

As I went upstairs to dress for the funeral, the relief I'd felt earlier was gone. Sally was right. Nothing had changed. She was still up the creek. And she still didn't have a paddle.

When Sally came in to have a cup of coffee before we went to the funeral, the paper was lying on the kitchen table. She picked it up and started reading aloud. There were signed messages of condolence from a local women's art co-operative and the Daughters of Bilitis. There was also a full-page ad from one of the fundamentalist churches containing a number of first-person accounts from men who described themselves as victims of pornography. All of them described exemplary boyhoods that ended abruptly when they were exposed to pornographic pictures and began to masturbate their way down the slippery slope to damnation.

When she had read the final confession, Sally slapped the paper down on the table.

"God, these guys are amazing. The old monkey-see-monkey-do theory of art and sex. Didn't the mums who taught these good boys ever tell them to keep their hands above the sheets?"

Angus, sitting opposite her, tried to look suave, as if he had conversations about masturbation at the breakfast table every day.

Sally seemed to dawdle over her coffee. I was the one who finally stood up and said it was time to go.

"My first all-girl funeral," Sally said to Angus as she zipped up her parka. He gave her a look that made me realize he was growing up.

It was a brilliant January morning, so cold there were sun dogs in the sky. We didn't talk much as we walked the few blocks to the campus. Classes started the next day, so there were students around with winter tans and new knapsacks and bags from the bookstore. On the signpost outside the University Women's Centre was an old poster with a picture of Paul McCartney and the word HELP in block letters above his head. Someone had drawn a balloon around it and given Paul some additional dialogue. "HELP – I'm old and boring," Paul said.

"No one can accuse Clea of that one any more," said Sally, and there was an edge to her voice that I should have picked up on, but didn't. In retrospect, it would have been better if Sally had not gone to the funeral. From the minute we walked up the steps to the women's centre, she was edgy and combative, and there was nothing inside that building to chill her out.

The women's centre was hot, and it had that egg-salad smell that seems to linger in all public buildings that serve short-order food. It was a pretty barren place: some posters on reproductive choice and date rape on the walls, and chairs arranged in semicircles with an aisle up the middle. By the time we arrived, almost all the chairs were full. Even so, the sister Sally sat next to ostentatiously got up and moved to the back of the room, and there was a nasty hissing sound from the people in the row behind us.

"Cows," Sally said under her breath. "So fucking self-righteous, so fucking precious about the place for women's art, but not one of them had the decency to ask if they could use my work on their little card here. Look at this." She tapped the front of the memorial card with one of her long, blunt fingers. It was a reproduction of a painting Sally had done in the early seventies: an adolescent girl sat legs apart, naked in front of the mirror over her dressing table. Her look, as she sat absorbed in the mystery of her body, was both radiant and fearful. The girl was Clea Poole.

"Not that I mind," Sally was saying, "but these women are always whining about being used by the power structure, you'd think one of them might understand the laws of copyright."

I started to say something, but at that moment, two women began to sing a cappella and the casket was brought in. It was covered in a quilt with a clitoral pattern, peach and ivory. All the pallbearers were women, and it stirred something in me to see them, strong and handsome, carrying a sister. When the singing ended, there was silence, then a thin woman in designer blue jeans and a white silk blouse came out of the front row, laid a hand on the casket and began to speak.

The thing you noticed first about Vivian Ludlow was her hair. She was younger than me, perhaps forty, but her hair was white, and she wore it shoulder length and extravagantly curled. It was very attractive. She was very attractive: good skin, no makeup, a full-lipped, sensitive mouth. She made no effort to raise her voice, yet she commanded that room.

"Like all of you here today, Clea Poole lived a life of risk and confrontation and inherent subversiveness," she began. "To be a woman is to live every day with the knowledge that the personal is political. It is to risk everything and to gain everything. It is to know the radically transgressive power of gender, but it is also to experience the moment of incarnation as self becomes flesh."

Beside me, Sally's voice was low with disgust. "They

think they invented it, you know. Clea made me go to a meeting once, and at the end the speaker jumped on the table and invited us all to have a peek at her uterus."

In spite of everything, I started to laugh. No one else was laughing. At the front, Vivian Ludlow was asking Clea's friends not to turn their eyes from the broken woman she was at the last because to do that was to devalue the purpose of Clea's life. Every eye in the place was on us now, and Sally was gazing back defiantly. Around us little brush fires of hostility were breaking out. At the front, Vivian Ludlow had moved to a safer topic, Clea's delight in Christmas, and I felt myself relax.

"Remember," Vivian Ludlow said softly, "how every year as the holidays began, Clea would make each of her friends a gingerbread house, small, perfectly crafted with love, an exquisite work by woman for woman, a reminder throughout that family time that we are family, too."

There was sobbing in the room. Beside me, Sally said in disgust, "And all she ever asked in return was that you crawl into the little gingerbread house with her and live happily ever after."

"Sal, for God's sake, shut up," I whispered. "You're going to get us lynched."

She glared at me, but she lapsed into silence until the pallbearers brought the casket down the aisle. On the way out, the other mourners gave us a wide berth, and as we left the women's centre and stepped into the brilliant January sunshine, I thought we were home free.

I was wrong. There was an old bus parked across the street from the centre, and as Sally and I stood on the steps, people began pouring out of it. They knew what they were doing. As they hit the street, a woman gave each of them a sign, and they crossed toward us. The messages on the signs were

Biblical, but the selections showed a distinct bias toward Old Testament retribution; verses about sin and punishment and death seemed to be the favourites.

"The revenge of the Righteous Protester," Sally said mildly, and she waved to them. They didn't wave back. Councillor Hank Mewhort was leading them. He was still wearing his "Silver Broom: Saskatoon '90" ski jacket, but the old green Hilltops tuque had been replaced by a tweed cap with ear flaps. The hat was an improvement, but the face under it was still smug and mean. He started to say something to Sally, but suddenly his jaw dropped and he fell silent. I turned to see what had stopped him.

Behind us, the doors of the women's centre had opened and the pallbearers were bringing out the casket. When I saw them, I knew why Hank Mewhort had frozen in his tracks. The pallbearers had changed their clothing. During the service, they had been wearing street clothes; now they were all in black – combat boots, skintight pants, leather jackets – and they were wearing gorilla masks, big toothy ones, the kind you pull right over your head.

Beside me, Sally snorted. "Just what this party needed, the Guerrilla Girls."

"What?" I said. The world was getting too complex for me.

"It's a political thing some women who make art in New York started. I guess these dopey souls think they're the road company. It's supposed to be a protest against tokenism and chauvinism and sexism and paternalism – all the isms. It's ridiculous, but of course Clea thought it was swell."

As the Guerrilla Girls loaded the casket into the hearse, Councillor Mewhort's friends stood dumbstruck. They looked as if they had seen the beast with seven horns and ten heads from Revelation. When the hearse pulled away, the Guerrilla Girls raised their leather-jacketed arms in a solemn salute.

Beside me Sally said, "Makes you proud to be a woman, doesn't it?"

One of the Guerrilla Girls heard her and she gave Sally the finger. Sally went over to her and ripped the mask from her face.

"I should have guessed you wouldn't miss out on this one, Anya," she said. "Look, why don't you do the art world a favour. Find some nice guy, settle down and forget about painting."

One of the other Guerrilla Girls reached toward Sally and shoved her.

"Cat fight," yelled Councillor Mewhort from the sidewalk. A Guerrilla Girl ran down the stairs and grabbed him by the collar. Then the fight was on. I didn't wait to see who won. It's hard to care about who wins a fight between moralists who want people to be struck down and feminists who wear animal heads to celebrate womanhood. Hank Mewhort had fallen to the sidewalk, and there were three Guerrilla Girls on top of him. Sally was trying to pull them away when I came up behind her, grabbed her by the arm and dragged her toward College Drive. I thought I heard a man's voice yell thanks at our retreating backs.

"Why were you trying to save him?" I asked.

"Three against one," said Sally. "Even if you're an asshole, those aren't fair odds."

I gave her shoulder a squeeze. Then without another word, we walked home.

The story has an addendum. That night after I'd driven home half of Angus's basketball team, I dug out my lecture notes for the next day and opened a bottle of Tuborg. Angus was having a shower, and Peter and Christy were downstairs studying. I went into the living room, put on an old recording of Dennis Brain playing the Mozart horn concertos and started to look over my introductory lecture. I had crossed out a couple of references that were no longer current and added a few that were when I heard someone at the front door. I looked out the window and saw Sally's Porsche at the curb.

It was a bitter night, and when I opened the door Sally walked past me into the house. She was carrying a packing case.

"Here," she said, leaning it against the wall, "this is for you. I'm sorry about this morning. I'm not much good when I feel cornered."

"I remember," I said.

She grinned. "Right. Anyway, open your present."

I started to wrestle with the box.

"I'll do it," she said. She bent over the box, and with a few strong, sure movements, she had it open and was holding the painting that had been inside.

"Let's take it into the light and see what you think," she said.

The picture took my breath away. Part of it, I guess, was seeing a piece of art that had a six-figure value casually propped against my kitchen wall, but the real impact came from the subject matter.

The scene was a tea party in the clearing down by the water at the Loves' summer cottage. The picture was suffused with summer light, that soft incandescence that comes when heat turns rain to mist. In the foreground there was a round table covered with a snowy cloth. On either side of the table was a wooden chair painted dark green. Nina Love was in one of the chairs. The eyelet sundress she was wearing was the colour of new ferns, and her skin was translucent. The light seemed to come through her flesh the way it comes through fine china. She was in profile, and the dark curve of her hair seemed to balance exactly the pale line of her features: yin and yang. Across the table from her sat a girl of fifteen, very tanned in a two-piece bathing suit that did nothing to hide a soft layer of baby fat. The girl's braided hair was bleached fair by the sun. Her expression as she watched Nina's graceful hands tilt the Limoges teapot was rapt – and familiar. The girl's face was my own thirty-two years before, and it glowed with admiration and love.

The woman and the girl bending toward one another over the luminous white cloth seemed enclosed in a private world. In the distance beyond them, the lake, blue as cobalt, lapped the shore.

There were other figures in the picture, and I knew them, too. Under the water, enclosed in a kind of bubble, were a man and a young girl. I could recognize the slope of Desmond Love's shoulders and the sweep of his daughter's blond hair as she bent over the fantastic sand castle they were building together in their little world under the waves.

Sally had been watching my face. Finally she said laconically, "Well?"

"It's incredible. I don't know what to say. The colours are wonderful – they seem to shimmer. And the way you've remembered us – not just the way we looked, but the way those days felt endless and hot . . ."

"And innocent," said Sally.

"Yes," I agreed, "and innocent. Sal, no one's ever given me a gift like this. I don't know what to say."

She smiled and made a gesture of dismissal.

"Does it have a title?" I asked.

"*Perfect Circles,*" Sally said.

"Yeah, I guess that's right, isn't it. You and Des in one circle and then Nina and me. God, I'd forgotten how I idolized her. It must have been awful for her to have this fat little girl hanging on her all the time."

"She loved it," said Sally. "She loved your need." And then she looked at me oddly. "I'm not being fair. Nina loved you, Jo. She still does. The one good thing I've ever been able to say about my mother is that she loves you."

"And you, Sal, if you'd let her."

For an answer she shrugged. "Anyway, if you ever decide to take up art, don't paint over this one. It's the only picture I ever did of Nina. She's so beautiful I can almost forgive her. Anyway, those were good summers."

"I can close my eyes still and see you and Des coming down the hill from the cottage with all the stuff you used to make your sand castles: shovels and trowels and spatulas and palette knives and sprinklers to keep the sand moist, and things to use as moulds and shapers. It always looked like you were going to work."

Sally smiled sadly. "We were. Des was a wonderful teacher. He was a wonderful artist. He was a wonderful father . . ." Her voice broke.

I looked up, surprised. "Hey, can I buy you a beer?"

"Sure," she said.

I went to the fridge and pulled out a cold Tuborg.

Sally checked the label carefully. "This one's okay. I won't spaz out on you." She snapped the cap off and held the bottle toward me. "To old times."

"To old times," I said.

For a while we were both silent. Then I said, "That picture brings so much back. You know, a couple of weeks ago Mieka asked me what happened between us, and when I tried to tell her, I thought I didn't really understand it myself."

"You were Nina's friend," she said simply.

"That's not fair," I said. "You were the one who went away. After Des died and you went away to New York to that art school, you vanished from my life."

"Is that what Nina told you?" Sally shook her head in

disbelief. "Jo, there was no art school. I never went to any school after I left Bishop Lambeth's."

"Come on. You were thirteen. You had to go school. That was the whole reason Nina let you move down there with Izaak Levin."

Sally roared. "Trust Nina to obey the letter if not the spirit of the truth. I guess I was at a school of the arts, except there was only one teacher, Izaak, and one pupil – me."

"What did you do?"

She took a long swallow of her Tuborg and set the bottle down in front of her.

"Well, the first year after Des died, I was pretty wrecked so we travelled most of the time – just drove around the U.S.A. in Izaak's shiny yellow convertible, seeing the sights, staying in motels."

"Sal, I don't believe a word of this. Why would a famous man like Izaak give up a year of his life to drive a thirteen-year-old girl around?"

She gave me a mocking smile.

"Sally, no. I know you said that you slept with him but . . . God, you were still a child. That's a pathology."

"Not such a child, Jo. It was a fair exchange. He got to have sex to his heart's content with a hot, young girl, and I got to see the U.S.A. in his Chevrolet. It worked out."

"How did you live?"

"Well, Izaak didn't have to work in burger joints to support us. He had quite a reputation in those days, and every so often he'd just sit down and make some phone calls. Then he'd go to some junior college or ladies' group, talk about art, pick up his cheque and we'd move along. He tried to make it interesting for me. You know, Vermont when the leaves changed and warm places in the winter. Once he did a class in San Luis Obispo for a month or so." She smiled at the memory. "Oh, Jo, we stayed at this motel that had fantasy rooms – a real fifties place – the court of Louis, jungle land, the wild west, that kind of thing." She shook her head and smiled. "Anyway, after a year we went to New York and Izaak wrote and went on TV and taught a bit, and I began to make art.

"I painted and we went to galleries and we fucked, and that was my school of the arts." She laughed. "Not a bad preparation, when you get right down to it, I guess. Anyway, that went on till I was about twenty. Things were getting ugly in the States – Johnson, Vietnam, all that stuff. Izaak said he'd stuck it out through McCarthy, but he'd had enough. We came to Saskatchewan for the Summer Art Colony at Emma Lake and we never went back."

"Sally, I'm incredulous. Where was Nina in all of this?"

She stood up. "Recovering from the tragic death of her husband," she said coldly. "Look, Jo, I've got to motor. I'm glad you like the painting."

I put my coat and boots on and followed her out to her car. I wanted the closeness to continue a little longer. As we walked down the driveway, our breath rose in ice fog around us. At the curb, the Porsche gleamed white in the moonlight, but as we got close to it, I noticed there was something wrong with the way it was positioned. It didn't take long to discover why. Someone had slashed the tires. Sally and I went around and checked them out. They had all been attacked, and whoever had done the slashing had done it over and over again. I felt a coldness in the pit of my stomach, and it didn't have anything to do with the weather.

"Sal, let's go back in and call the police," I said.

She looked into the heavens. "Full moon tonight – Looney-Tunes time. The cops are going to be busy chasing down people whose eyeteeth have started to grow. They won't get to us for hours." She hugged herself against the cold. "So, Jo, it looks like you're going to have to ask me for a sleepover."

"Done," I said. And we trudged through the snow to the warmth of the house.

# CHAPTER

8

On the tenth of January I finished my class on populist politics and the Saskatchewan election of '82 and walked across campus to my office in the arts building. From habit, I slowed up in front of the room where English 250 met. Mieka had been taking that class before Christmas, and it had always given me a nice feeling to walk by and see her sitting at her desk by the window, chewing the end of her pen, looking thoughtful. The desk by the window was empty now; Mieka hadn't come back to university after the break. During the hours in which she should have been learning about Alice Munro and Sinclair Ross, she was stripping woodwork at the Old Court House and talking to suppliers. Her decision didn't please me much.

When I walked through my office door, the phone was ringing. It was Sally, and what she had to say didn't please me much, either.

"Jo, do you have any free time this afternoon?" She was silent for a beat. "There's news."

"I have to pick up Angus's skates over on Main Street –

the sharpener's near the Broadway Café. I can meet you there in fifteen minutes."

"The Broadway'll be fine. I'm at Izaak's now just around the corner."

"Sal, is the news good?"

When she answered, she sounded infinitely weary. "Is it ever?" she asked.

It was a grey, sleety day, and the only parking place I could find was three blocks from the restaurant. By the time I walked through the front door, I was chilled to the bone and apprehensive, but the Broadway Café was a welcoming place for the cold and the lonely. It looked the way I imagined the café looked in Hemingway's story "A Clean, Well-Lighted Place": a shining counter with stools down one side of the room; dark wooden booths upholstered in wine-coloured leather down the other. The walls were covered with mirrors and blowups of pictures of old movie stars. Sally was sitting in a back booth under a palely tinted Fred Astaire.

When she saw me, she smiled wanly. "They found my gun," she said without preamble. "Some kids were tobogganing down by the river and they found a gun and took it to the police. They say it's the one that did the murders."

The waitress came over and poured coffee for us. When she left, I turned to Sally.

"Okay, start at the beginning."

Her hair was loose around her shoulders, and she ran her hands through it in a gesture of frustration. "Tell me where the beginning is, Jo, because I don't know any more. Do you know how often I've been down to the cop shop? But until this morning I thought it was all going to go away. It seemed as if everything was in limbo. Nothing got better, but nothing got worse, either. Well, now something has gotten worse. And, Jo, nothing's gotten better: the police haven't found the tape that was in the video camera at the gallery the night Clea was killed. They haven't even got a sniff about who it was Kyle chased down the river bank. And I still don't have an alibi."

"Have the police stopped looking for the man in the ski mask?" I asked.

"Mary Ross McCourt says they haven't, but now that they've got the gun, I wonder how hard they're going to look. There are just too many pieces falling into place."

Sally took a sip of coffee and closed her eyes. She looked exhausted.

"Are you okay?" I asked.

"Just great," she said. "I've got the police breathing down my neck from nine to five, and when they go off duty, the merry pranksters are in there cranking up the action."

"Oh, no, I thought that would be over by now," I said.

"Well, you thought wrong," she said flatly. "It's still, as they say, a happening thing. Most of it's just head games: eggs frozen on the windshield in the morning, sugar in the gas tank, lipstick love letters on the windows of my studio. But it's getting to me. I'm giving up. Tomorrow, I'm moving into an apartment in the Park Towers, you know the ones, downtown by the Bessborough. Stu has a friend in the penthouse who's in Florida for the winter. This guy likes to think of himself as a patron of the arts, so he didn't mind me using his place."

"Probably gets off on the idea of the notorious Sally Love sleeping in his bed," I said.

For the first time that afternoon she laughed. "Probably. But it's nice, and there's a swimming pool for Taylor when she visits. Anyway, I should give you my number there." She wrote it down on a napkin and handed it to me with a sigh. "God, I wish this was all over. But it will be soon. And when I can get working again, I'll be okay. Good old Stu found me some studio space at the university. I've already moved my stuff in."

"Sounds like Stu's turned chivalrous now that you're a lady in distress."

"Well, it might be something a little less – is the word *altruistic*? – anyway, a little more selfish than chivalry. Stu's got this book on my art coming out in the spring, and I think he's worried I'm not going to like it. He's already puffing out his chest and talking about how art thrives on diverse critical approaches . . ."

"Which means?" I asked.

"Which means that what he's written is a crock and he's terrified I'm going to blow the whistle on him."

"But you wouldn't," I said.

"Jo, this is serious. It isn't personal. It's not about me. It's about what I do. If it's stupid, I'll have to say so."

"Well," I said, "for everyone's sake, let's hope it isn't stupid."

"Right," she said, standing up and pulling on her coat "Let's hope it isn't stupid. And let's hope that guy who was trying to give me a flat the night of the murder decides he'll give me an alibi if I give him his tuque back, and let's hope my terrorists get frostbite or writer's cramp and leave me alone." She shrugged. "Hey, let's go crazy and wish for it all. Maybe for once life will work out."

I followed her toward the front of the restaurant. Halfway to the cash register Sally stopped and looked up at a picture on the wall. It was an old poster advertising *The Misfits* with Clark Gable, Marilyn Monroe and Montgomery Clift.

"All dead," said Sally.

"But we remember them," I said, "through their movies."

She gave me the old mocking Sally smile. "That doesn't make them any less dead," she said.

I picked up Angus's skates and headed to Ninth Street and my car. When I looked at the house I'd parked in front of, it seemed familiar. It was a pleasant unexceptional place: two-storey, white clapboard. With a start, I realized it was Izaak Levin's house. I'd looked him up in the book after I saw him the night of Sally's opening. I'd even driven by. I told myself I might need to know where he lived for future reference.

There hadn't been any need for future reference. When I'd spoken to him the morning after Sally's opening, Izaak Levin had promised to call in the new year, and he had – twice. The first time, I had already arranged to have dinner with an old political friend. The second time Izaak called was after Sally had told me what had happened between them in the months after Des died. It took real restraint to keep from banging the receiver down and blowing out his eardrum.

I was just about to pull away when Izaak's front door opened and a woman in a black mink coat came hurrying out. She had her head down, but I knew the coat and I knew the woman. It was Nina Love. She didn't see me. She turned and walked toward a car I recognized immediately as Stu's Mercedes. I watched the licence plate as she drove up the street. ARTS 1 it said. So it wasn't Stu's car; it was the car that had belonged to Sally when she and Stu were together. His was the twin of this one, but his licence read ARTS 2. "Grounds enough for divorce in those licence plates alone," Sally said blandly when she told me about them.

There was no mistaking the car or the woman. I turned off the ignition and walked up the front path to Izaak Levin's house. He answered the door almost immediately. It was apparent when he opened the door that he had expected to see Nina again. He even looked past me, to see if she was still there.

"She's gone," I said, "but I'm here. May I come in?"

Without a word, he stood aside, and I walked past him. He was holding a manila envelope. It was sealed. When he saw me looking at the envelope, he shoved it into the drawer of a little table in the entrance hall. Not very trusting.

"Well," he said finally, "this is a welcome surprise. The last time we talked, I thought I discerned a chill. Come in and sit down. Can I get you something? A drink perhaps, or there's fresh coffee."

"Coffee would be fine," I said as I followed him into the living room. If I'd known what was waiting for me there, I would have chosen the drink. When I looked around Izaak Levin's living room, I knew I was at an exhibition curated by an obsessive. I was standing in the middle of a gallery of Sally Love – of art made not by her, but about her. Sally in all her ages, all her moods, seen by different eyes, transmuted into art by a hundred pairs of hands working with differing techniques in different media.

The walls were filled with paintings of her, and the floor was stacked with more. To get my bearings, I sat in the first chair I came to. Propped against the wall beside me, a sepia Sally, all halftones except for the brilliant red of her mouth, licked a sensuous upper lip; next to it, a pastel Sally's virginal profile glowed in a spring garden; on the coffee table in front of me a ceramic Sally holding a cat sprawled on a rocker. Sally was everywhere in that room, and even I knew the art was wonderful. But the effect was not wonderful; it was eerie, like the rooms you see on TV after a psychopath has committed a crime.

When Izaak came in from the kitchen carrying a tray with coffee and a bottle of brandy, I jumped.

He smiled. "Maybe you should have a little of this in your coffee," he said, holding up the bottle.

"No, thanks," I said, "I'm just a little overwhelmed by your collection. How did it come about?"

He handed me my coffee. "Sally did the first one herself – that one over the mantelpiece, the one where she's sitting on the hood of the old Chevy. It was a kind of joke. When she first came to study with me, I called her an academy of one. Someone told her that when artists are admitted to the American Academy in New York, they have to give the academy a self-portrait. Sally painted that picture for my birthday. She was fourteen. The others just came over the years. Sally is such an exceptional subject; people who make art are drawn to her."

I put down my cup and walked over to look more closely at Sally's self-portrait. It would have been easy to dismiss that picture because, at first glance, it seemed so stereotypical: a fifties magazine ad for a soft drink or suntan lotion. A pretty girl wearing a halter top and shorts hugged one knee and extended the other leg along the hood of a yellow convertible – a glamorous pose, sex with a ponytail. But Sally had used colour to create light in an odd and disturbing way. The car glowed magically surreal – it was a car to take you anywhere, and the hot pink stucco of the motel behind the girl panted with lurid life. Sally herself was a cutout, a conventional calendar girl without life or dimension, an object in someone else's world of highways and clandestine sex.

I turned and looked at Izaak Levin. "And what did you make of that picture when she gave it to you?"

He looked at me quizzically. "Do you mean as a piece of art?"

"No," I said, reaching over and pouring a little brandy into my coffee cup, "as a young girl's self-assessment. What would you think was going on in the mind and heart of a fourteen-year-old who saw herself like that?" The image of the woman that child had become floated up and lodged in my mind

("Maybe for once life will work out"), and I was surprised at the rage in my voice. "You understand, I'm not asking you this as an art critic, I'm asking you as a human being."

He was silent.

"I'm waiting," I said.

His glass still had a couple of ounces of brandy in it, and he drank them down and shuddered. "How much," he said finally, "do you know about Sally and me?"

"Everything, I guess."

"Joanne, no one knows everything." His voice was so soft I had to lean forward to hear it. A private voice.

"Sally told me you were lovers," I said, "and that it started when she was thirteen."

"And you're appalled."

"Yes. I'm appalled. Thirteen! My God, Izaak. You were what? Forty? Her father had just died. Didn't certain patterns suggest themselves to you?"

I thought he was a weakling who would be devastated by someone else knowing the truth about what he had done. He wasn't. He looked at me steadily.

"The circumstances were unusual. Joanne, don't judge us yet. How much do you remember about the time after Des Love died?"

"The time immediately after? Everything. I don't think you remember, but I was there that night. Sally and I were going to a birthday dance across the lake. Nina was going to take us across as soon as you got back with the boat. Anyway, I went back to our cottage to change my shoes, and that made me late getting to the Loves'. But I was there just after you found them. I'll remember every second of that night till the day I die."

He pulled a cigarette from a fresh pack of Camels and placed it between his lips. He didn't light it.

"I remembered a girl being there," he said. "I didn't know it was you. So you've carried your own burden of memory all these years."

"Yes," I said, "I have, and what made it worse was I lost Sally, too. After that night I didn't see her again for years. They wouldn't let me see her in the hospital. And then – well, she was supposed to be away at school."

"But she wasn't," Izaak finished for me. He lit his cigarette and splashed more brandy in his glass. He was, I realized, well on his way to being drunk. "And now, Joanne," he said, "I'm going to try to mute your hostility. Are you mutable?"

"Try me," I said.

He laughed thinly. "Well, as they say, it was a dark and stormy night – the night after Des's funeral, to be precise. Owing to circumstances, the funeral had been particularly grisly, and I was sitting in my living room trying to get drunk. I lived not far from the Wellesley Hospital, which, of course, was where they had taken Des's family. There was a knock at the door, and when I opened it, Sally was there. She was in terrible shape. She hadn't been discharged. She had just put on her coat and walked out.

"'I won't go back to that house,' she said, 'and I won't go back to her.' She was soaked to the skin, and I went upstairs to run a hot bath and get her some dry clothes. When I came down, the bottle of whisky on the coffee table – a bottle which, incidentally, I had just nicely started – was just about empty. Fortunately, Sally's stomach rebelled. I got her upstairs to the bathroom in time, but while she was retching into the toilet bowl, somehow her jaw locked open – I suppose like a hinge that's pushed back too far.

"At any rate, there I was with a drunken thirteen-year-old, no relation to me, in a hospital gown and in need of help. I started to call a cab so I could get her to an emergency ward somewhere, but the idea of going back to the hospital made her wild. She started clawing at the phone and at me and making the most godawful sounds. So I slapped her – the movie cure for hysteria." He dragged gratefully on the Camel. "Luckily, the slap unlocked the jaw. I undressed her, put her in the tub and went out in the hall and sat on the floor outside the bathroom door listening until she came out, and I knew she was safe." He smiled to himself. "Or as safe as any of us ever are."

I was stunned. "Sally made it sound like such a lark – an adventure," I said weakly.

He picked up the ceramic figure of Sally with the cat and ran his forefinger along the curve of Sally's body. "She was a very wounded girl. That first year was a time of convalescence for her."

"With you as doctor. Where was Nina in all of this?"

He shrugged. "Where is she ever? Taking care of Nina." He looked hard at me, "I can see I have just made your hostility less mutable. So be it. To answer your question, Nina was enthusiastically in favour of dumping Sally on my doorstep. Sally and I went to Nina's hospital room together to ask. It took Nina an excruciating one-tenth of a millisecond to accede to our request."

He pronounced his words with exaggerated care. I knew the alcohol was beginning to blunt his responses, but I couldn't let the slur against Nina go unanswered.

"Be fair, Izaak. Nina had just endured a situation that went beyond nightmare."

"Our nightmares arise out of our deepest fears and longings," he said gently. "And no matter what, Sally was her daughter."

"And you," I said, fighting tears, "were the man Nina chose to act as a father for her child. In loco parentis – isn't that the phrase? Damn it, Izaak, you can't shift the blame for what you did to Nina. You were the one who took advantage.

You were the one who violated the trust." I picked up my coat and started to leave.

He followed me to the front hall. For the first time that day I noticed that he was limping, and at some not very admirable level, I was glad. I was glad he had hurt himself. The phone rang and he went to answer it. I couldn't hear much of what he said. I heard the phrases, "That won't be necessary, the need is past," and then he lowered his voice and I couldn't make out the words, but I could hear that he was speaking. The drawer to the table in the entrance hall was open a little. I pulled it out and picked up the manila envelope. I could still hear Izaak Levin's voice in the kitchen, low, indistinct. I shook the envelope the way children do on Christmas morning with their packages and then decided the hell with it. I ripped the flap back a little. Not far, just enough to see that inside was a roll of bills that would choke a horse.

I put the envelope back and carefully shut the drawer. When I got in the car, I was surprised to see I was shaking – coffee or guilt, I didn't know which. I sat there for a minute, taking deep breaths, calming down. Finally, I put the key in the ignition. But before I pulled out into the street, I took one last look at Izaak Levin's house. He was standing in the doorway, elegant, worldly as ever in his tweed jacket and horn-rimmed glasses. In one hand he had the brandy bottle, but he used the other to give me a mocking salute.

# CHAPTER

# 9

As I stopped for the light at Broadway, I was trying to work it all out. What had Nina been doing at Izaak Levin's? They had known one another for years, but their relationship was hardly cordial. And where had the money come from? Nina had told me that Izaak had chronic money problems, but the roll of bills I had seen in that envelope went well beyond what you kept around in case the paperboy came to collect. Sally had been there earlier, but if she had taken the money over as part of a business transaction, why was it in cash? And why did Izaak still have the envelope in his hand, unopened, half an hour after she left? Questions. I looked at my watch. There was time before Angus came home from school to stop by Nina's and get some answers.

The light changed and I pulled into the intersection. Across the street I could see Angus's mecca: 7 Eleven, Home of the Big Gulp. As I pulled onto Broadway, I felt rather than saw a car coming toward me. By the time I turned to look at it, I only had time to know three things for certain: the car coming at me was big, it was green, and it wasn't going to stop.

The next thing I knew I was lying on my back in a room that smelled of medicine, and a black man with a gentle voice was asking me if I knew my name. When I told him, he nodded approvingly. "And what did you have for breakfast today, Jo?" I knew that, too. "And the day of the week?" Right again. He looked pleased. Obviously, I was a promising student. I also knew the names of the prime minister and of the premier of my province. Head of the class.

"Well, you're salvageable," he said with a smile. "We're going to patch you up a bit now," and then I felt a pinprick in my arm, and I drifted off. I remember an elevator and a room where Debussy was playing, and there was a bright light over my head and the same gentle voice that had asked me to name the prime minister was saying something about garlic. And then a woman was saying, "Joanne, Joanne, time to wake up. Come on, Joanne, take a deep breath. Get the oxygen in." Then I was in a bed and Mieka's Greg was standing over me.

Panicked, I fought my way back to consciousness. "Is Mieka okay? And the boys?"

He held my hand. "Everybody's okay, including you. You were in a car accident."

"Nobody was . . . ?" I asked.

"Nobody was hurt but you and the Volvo. You're going to be fine."

I felt a rush of relief and gratitude. "Greg, thank you. Thank you for everything."

"Jo, I didn't do anything."

I smiled at him. "You're here. I'm here." And then an inspiration. "Hey, Greg, remember what Woody Allen says? 'Eighty per cent of success is showing up.'"

He laughed, and safe again, I felt my limbs grow heavy and I drifted off to sleep.

To sleep and to dream. I was walking down a corridor in

the hospital, looking for the way out. But the corridors were arranged oddly, like a maze. I knew I was going in circles and I could feel the gathering of panic. Then I came to a big double door marked AUTHORIZED PERSONNEL ONLY. I pushed the door open. There was a vast room, empty except for an eight-sided desk in the middle. In the centre of the desk was a well, and Izaak Levin was seated there. "I can't find my way," I said. "Right or left?" he said. "What?" I said. "Conscious or unconscious," he said irritably. "Left," I said. "You'll be sorry," he said. But I'd already started through the doors at the left. I knew at once that I was in the old wing of the building, the one that no one used any more. All along the corridors the doors to rooms were open. The patients' rooms were empty. The medical rooms had things in them that I remembered from my father's office thirty years before. Finally I came to the sunroom that had been in the Wellesley Hospital when my father was on staff there. The room was filled with the furniture that I recognized at once as coming from the Loves' old cottage. Nina was there, wearing her black mink coat, but she must have been a nurse because she was pouring medicine into glasses. She didn't see me. And then Sally was there, not Sally as she was now, but Sally at fourteen in her nightgown. She was pushing a gurney, very purposefully. There was a body on it covered with a green sheet.

When she saw Nina, she hissed at me urgently, "Jo, you should have turned right. You can still get out, but you'll have to leave her behind." I turned to tell Nina where I was going but she was in another room counting money. Then Sally and I ran along the corridors of the abandoned wing till we came to the part of the building that was still used. I could feel my apprehension lighten. "You can look now," Sally said, pointing to the figure on the gurney. I didn't want to, but I knew I had to. I grabbed the corner of the sheet and

pulled it back in one quick gesture. There on the stretcher
was Woody Allen. He sat up and rubbed the bridge of his
nose. "Eighty per cent of life consists of just showing up, Jo,"
he said.

I started to laugh, and when I woke up I was laughing
and Mieka was there laughing and looking worried at the
same time.

"Well," she said, "no need to ask you if you're glad to be
back from the jaws of death. It looks like you were having a
lot of fun in there." Then she hugged me. "Mum, we were
so scared."

"I know," I said.

She started to cry. "I love you."

"I love you, too," I said. "So how's the catering business
coming?"

She told me. And after a while Peter came and told me
about a summer job possibility with a veterinarian down in
the southwest of the province. Then Angus came and told
me that three guys from the Oilers were going to be in the
mall signing autographs on Saturday and if he donated fifty
dollars to the Hockey Oldtimers he could have breakfast
with them. And then a nurse said a plastic surgeon wanted
to check my forehead and anyway I'd had enough visitors for
one day. She shooed the kids away. Then after the doctor
left, she came back and tucked me in for the night.

I couldn't sleep. I lay there listening to hospital sounds.
Then the lights were turned down in the hall and I was alone
in the half light. At first, when I saw Sally in the doorway, I
thought I was dreaming. She put her finger to her lips, then
moved quickly toward the head of the bed where she
couldn't be seen by anyone passing by.

When she leaned over to give me a hug, I could smell the
cold fresh air on her. She looked at the cuts on my face
critically.

"How bad are they?" she asked.

"Not bad at all," I said, "except for the one on my forehead, and it's manageable. A plastic surgeon was just in here. He said that I'll be 'scarred but not disfigured' – that's a direct quote. He also said I'm lucky I have bangs because they'll cover the scar."

Sally shook her head. "Good news all around, eh?"

"Right. Oh, Sally, it's so good to see you. But how did you ever get by the nurse?"

She opened her coat. There was a picture ID pinned to her blouse. "I flashed this at her. Said I was a specialist from St. Paul's."

I laughed. "Where'd you get it?"

"One of Stu's loonier ideas a couple of years ago. Everyone with access to the vaults at the Mendel had to have an ID. Anyway, for once something Stu did actually worked out. It came in handy tonight." Suddenly, she was serious. "I had to see you, Jo. When Mieka called to tell me you were okay, I was so relieved, and then I just started to shake."

"That's about how I felt," I said. "It's not much fun to see how easily it can all end."

She sat down carefully on the bed beside me. In the shadowy light, her face looked both older and younger. "But you can't think about that," she said. "You can't think about how quickly it can be over, or you'll be too paralyzed to live. There's no point in being afraid of dying. It's going to happen. What we should be scared of is blowing the here and now."

"Carpe diem?" I asked.

She raised her eyebrows questioningly.

"Seize the day," I said.

"Seize the day," she repeated softly. "That's it. Because nobody knows how many days we have. I've never thought much about any of this stuff before. I've always just done what I wanted to do – made art. But Taylor's changed everything.

Jo, she is so talented. She is going to be so good. And she needs a good teacher. She needs me to do for her what Des did for me. Keep her from getting dicked around."

She stood up and walked over to the window. I could see her profile as she looked down at the lights of the city. "I'm not going to wait any more. Lately I've let everybody but me call the shots – the police, Stu, Nina, even the merry pranksters. But that's over. I'm getting on with it. I'm going to Vancouver tomorrow morning. My lawyer says since I haven't been charged with anything, the police here can't stop me. I'm going to look for a house for Taylor and me." She turned to face me. "You're sure it's okay with you if I leave."

"I'm sure."

"Do you want me to leave you the keys to my car? Mieka says the Volvo's done for."

"Are you sure you trust me to drive after today?"

She smiled. "I trust you. And since you're being so brave, I'll bring you a present. What's B.C. got that you want?"

"Pussy willows – the fat kind. I want an armful."

She sighed. "You know, Jo, sometimes you're just too wholesome for words." Then she bent down and kissed my forehead. "Did I ever tell you I love you?"

I felt a lump in my throat. "No, but now that you have, I may get you to put it in writing." For a moment I couldn't speak. Then I said, "I love you, too, Sally."

She grinned. "Good. Look, Jo, I've got to motor. I'll call you from Vancouver and tell you all about the boys on the beach." She gave my foot a squeeze and she was gone. Five minutes later I fell asleep. Despite the bruises, stitches and bandages, I was smiling.

I awakened the next morning to the smell of coffee and the sounds of carts loaded with breakfast trays being rolled along the hall. When I swung my legs over the side of the bed and sat up, I felt lightheaded, but I was determined to make it to the bathroom. There was a mirror above the sink and when I saw my face, I wished I'd stayed in bed. My forehead was hidden by a surgical bandage, both my eyes were black, and there was bruising across my cheekbones.

"You've never been at your best in the morning," I said to my reflection, then I hobbled to the safety of bed.

Breakfast was a lukewarm boiled egg, toast and margarine, dry cereal with room-temperature milk and a glass of Quench. Still, I was alive. Being ugly, being fed a meal prepared by the dieticians from hell didn't change that. I was alive, and as I sat watching the political panel on *Good Morning, Canada* I was happy.

Nina was my first visitor of the day. She came by just after breakfast, bringing the novel that was at the top of the *New York Times* best-seller list and a pink azalea, heavy with blooms. When she saw my face, I could see her muscles tense. She didn't like sickness. It was, I knew, an effort of will for her to come into a hospital. She embraced me affectionately, but I noticed that when she sat down, she pulled the visitor's chair well away from the bed.

We talked a little about the accident, and then Nina told me that Sally had flown to Vancouver that morning. She didn't try to hide her anger.

"This is why she drives people crazy. All these spur of the moment decisions as if no one exists in the world but Sally Love. She had promised to take Taylor up to the university and show her the studio today."

"Was Taylor upset?" I asked.

Nina hesitated. "Well, no. Sally called her and seemed to explain things to Taylor's satisfaction, but that's not the point."

"What is the point then, Ni? If Taylor's happy and Sally's happy, why does it matter?" I spoke more sharply than I intended to, and Nina looked surprised and wounded.

"You don't think I have a right to involve myself?"

"No, Ni, of course you have a right to be involved. It's just I don't think you're being fair to Sally. She came by here last night, and I think I understand why she felt she needed to go to Vancouver. This hasn't been the greatest time for her, you know."

"But it's been great for the rest of us?" Nina asked icily.

My head was starting to ache. "I know it's been hard for everyone." I took a deep breath. "Nina, there's something I need to ask you about. In fact, I was on my way to talk to you when I had the accident."

She stiffened. I tried to choose words that weren't threatening. "Yesterday afternoon I had an errand over on Broadway. I was parked in front of Izaak Levin's house. I saw you coming out of there, and after you left, I went in and talked to him."

At first, it seemed as if she hadn't heard me. She was wearing a heavy silver bracelet of linked Siamese cats. While I was talking, the catch had sprung open and she seemed, for a while, to be wholly absorbed in the problem of fastening it again. Finally, she looked up.

"What did he tell you?" she asked.

"Just things about the past," I said.

She seemed to relax. "I wouldn't believe everything Izaak Levin tells you, Jo. He's not a very nice man."

I could feel a pressure behind my right eye. "Damn it, Nina, if he wasn't very nice why did you let your thirteen-year-old daughter move in with him?"

She was alert again. "So that's it. Do you think it was easy for me? You were there, Jo. You remember how it was. She didn't want any part of me. Your father said it was because I reminded her of what she had lost in Des. He urged me to let her go." She reached out and covered my hand with her own. Her hand was cool and smooth, and I thought how often that hand had reached out to reassure me.

"I had you, Jo," she said. "And that made all the difference. It was a fair exchange. Your mother didn't want you, and Sally didn't want me. I had to come up with a solution that was right for everyone. It wasn't easy; you know that. You saw how much Sally's defection hurt me. But it had to happen."

I looked at her perfect heart-shaped face. "Ni, how can someone who looks as fragile as you do be so strong?"

She looked pleased. "Do you know that old Chinese proverb: 'The sparrow is small, but it contains all the vital organs of the elephant'?" She stood up and started to put her coat on. "I think you've had enough for one day. You look a little weary. Next time, let's leave the past in the past, and talk about all the things convalescent women are supposed to talk about."

"Such as?"

Her smile was impish. "Such as Easter bonnets and where hemlines arc going to be in the spring and the best place in town to get a bikini wax."

My head was pounding. "That sounds so good, and we'll do it next time, I promise. But there's one more thing, and I have to know this. Nina, did you give Izaak some money yesterday – a lot of money in a manila envelope?"

The cat bracelet slipped from her wrist and clattered noisily onto the floor. For a beat, we both looked at it in horror, as if it were a living thing. Nina bent to pick it up. She fastened it carefully, then she looked at me. I couldn't read the expression on her face, but her tone was urgent.

"Jo, you must promise me that what I tell you won't leave this room. The money was from Stuart. I was just the messenger. He'd die if he knew you'd found out. No one must know about this. If it gets out, it will destroy Stuart, and he and Taylor have suffered so much already." She had tears in her eyes.

"My God, Nina, what has Stuart done?"

"He wrote a book, Jo. That's all he did, but he's so anxious about its reception that he struck a kind of bargain with Izaak. Izaak agreed to give favourable attention to the book in print and send copies to his colleagues in the art world along with a flattering letter."

Suddenly I was so tired I could barely hold my head up. All I wanted to do was sleep. But I had shaken out the bag of tricks and I had to stay there until all the surprises were accounted for.

"And what did Stu agree to do for Izaak?" I asked.

"You know the answer to that already, Jo. You saw it yesterday afternoon. In exchange for friendly consideration, Stuart agreed to extricate Izaak from his latest financial crisis."

"This doesn't make sense, Nina. If the book's so bad, there'll be other reviews. Stuart can't buy off everybody."

"The book's brilliant, Jo, but you know how these things are. Izaak's always been considered the expert on Sally's work. People will take their lead from him. A good response is crucial. Stuart's going to be fifty years old this summer. He sees this book as his chance to make his mark professionally." She sat on the bed in the same place where her daughter had sat twelve hours earlier. "Jo, please don't say anything. Stuart's been wounded enough. If this came out . . ."

"He'd be a laughingstock," I said.

She winced. "Or worse. Please, Jo."

I sighed. "I won't say anything, Nina. You've asked me not to, and that's all I need." Suddenly I was exhausted. "But I think you're right. I think I should sleep now."

She plumped up my pillows and smoothed my sheet. Then she blew me a kiss and moved quietly out of the room. This time, when I fell asleep I wasn't smiling.

When I woke up, there was a small green wicker basket on the nightstand. Inside was a bagel with cream cheese and lox, a bottle of soda, a century pear and a piece of wicked-looking chocolate cake. There was a white silk bow on the basket and a card. "Judgements," the card said. Mieka's name and a phone number were printed in the lower right-hand corner. On the back she had scrawled, "Eat and be well. Love, M." I ate and felt better.

Hilda McCourt came by just as the one o'clock news came on the radio. She was wearing a skiing outfit, lime green and cerise, very Scandinavian in design. It looked expensive enough for Aspen. Her bright red hair was tucked under a lime-green ski cap, and her cheeks were rosy from the cold. In that room that smelled of disinfectant and medicine, she was bright with health. She pulled up a chair by my bed, sat down and bent close to look at my face.

"It could have been a great deal worse," she said thoughtfully. "I've had your name put on the prayer roster at the cathedral. We're thanking God for your deliverance, not praying for your recovery."

"I've been doing some thanksgiving myself," I said.

"I expect you have," she said. "Well, let's get on with life. Shall I bring you up to date on the gallery's celebration for Sally Love?"

"You're going to have to do more than bring me up to date on it," I said. "I didn't even know it was happening."

She looked puzzled. "I stopped by your house last week and left some information with your younger son."

"Angus?" I said. "He's the black hole of messages."

"I'll bear that in mind next time," she said. "At any rate, the affair for Sally is going to be on February fourteenth. I couldn't resist the Eros-love-Valentine connection, and, of course, we had to speed things up because Sally told me she and her daughter are leaving town. It's going to be a glitter-ing evening, Joanne. Black tie, of course, with a sit-down dinner prepared by a first-rate caterer."

"I suppose you already have a caterer," I said.

"Yes, all that's been taken care of. Did you have someone in mind?"

"Maybe for next time," I said, smiling.

"Well, as I said, there'll be dinner. But here's the treat, and it was Sally's idea. She's agreed to let us auction off the preliminary sketches for the sexual parts in the fresco in Erotobiography. It's a wonderful tie-in with Valentine's Day. And an auction will be a feather in the cap for the gallery, not to mention a solid moneymaker. We've already had some nibbles from the national media interested in a Valentine story with a twist. Stuart is thrilled with all the attention."

"Hilda, how long have you known Stu?"

She looked surprised. "He was my pupil when he was in high school, and, of course, I knew his parents."

"What do you think of him?"

"That's an odd question," she said, "but I presume not an idle one, so I'll be candid. I think Stuart Lachlan is a pleasant but weak man. He's good company but not the man you'd want with you in a foxhole. Do you want to hear more?"

"Yes," I said, "I think I do."

"I'll give you a little family history, then. Stuart was an only child. His parents were wealthy, at least by Saskatoon standards, and his mother doted on him. I bristle at those who blame all their difficulties in life on their mothers, but in Stuart's case it would be justified. Caroline Lachlan pro-tected her son so rigorously that she emasculated him.

"I remember when he was in grade eleven he received a poor mark on an essay. Caroline came up to the school to castigate me. She told me that Stuart's understanding of the play was deeper than mine and she was taking his paper up to the chairman of the drama department at the university to have it 'assessed by a qualified person.'"

"Did she do it?"

"Of course. That night when I was at home, my phone rang. Gordon Barnes was chairman of the drama department in those days. He was a dear man, but he did not suffer fools gladly, even rich ones. When I picked up the phone, he was on the other end. 'The mark is not altered,' he boomed, and that was the end of it."

I laughed. "Poor Stu."

"Indeed," said Hilda. She leaned a little closer. "And Joanne, do you know the title of the play that Stuart's mother thought he had done such a bang-up job on?"

I shook my head.

"*Oedipus Rex.*"

We both laughed, and then Hilda grew serious. "It is funny in the telling. But when you think of what Stuart became, the story's not so funny. Graham Greene has a splendid line in *The Power and The Glory*: 'There is always one moment in childhood when the door opens and lets the future in.' I wonder if that was Stuart's moment?" Her eyes looked sad. "I don't think Stuart ever had a chance to develop any moral muscle. Caroline was always there, running interference, and her son became a man who has no ability to deal with adversity because he never had to. You saw him when Sally left him. He just about destroyed himself with liquor. Luckily for everyone, Sally's mother came along and Stuart had someone to lean on again. She's much the same type as Caroline, you know."

I thought I'd misheard her. "Nina and Stu's mother? Oh, no, Hilda, you're wrong there. Nina has her faults, but . . ." Pain stabbed the place behind my stitches. It was the first time I'd ever articulated a criticism of Nina.

Hilda looked at me curiously. "I'm always willing to be convinced, but not at this moment. Right now, I want to talk about you. How long are they keeping you in here?"

"The doctors say a few more days. They also say I can teach on Monday. The way my face looks, I may wear a mask. The plastic surgeon says no makeup till all the cuts are healed. I hope I look a little less horrifying by the night of Sally's party."

"You'll be fine. You're in good health. You'll heal quickly." She stood up. "Now, if there's anything at all I can do to help, let me know. And when you're up to snuff again, you can help me. I need a fresh eye to help me shop. I'm having a terrible time finding a dress for Sally's gala. Everything seems too trendy. I like a sense of fun in daytime clothes, but when I get an evening gown, I want to get one I can wear for years."

She zipped up her ski jacket and disappeared down the hall – more than eighty years old and determined to find a party dress she could really get some mileage out of.

Two days later I was discharged from the hospital. The cuts in my forehead would be a long time healing, but the bruises under my eyes were fading, and the cuts on my cheek were distinctly better. Most importantly, I felt fine. Mieka had continued with what she called her "test runs"; three times a day something freshly prepared and tasty would arrive in the distinctive green Judgements wicker basket. There was a half bottle of wine with dinner. It was food to get well for, and I did.

On the day I was discharged, a package came to me by courier from Vancouver. Inside was a bubble-gum pink sweatshirt, with *I LOVE JO* written across the chest in sequins and bugle beads. In Sally's surprisingly precise hand there was a note: "Now you've got it in writing. Get well soon. Love and XXX, S."

I wore the sweatshirt home from the hospital. As Peter pulled into the driveway, I could see the dogs waiting at the front window. Inside, Angus had a bed made up for me on the couch in the den, and the morning paper was open at the TV page. As I pulled the afghan around my chin and settled in to watch the local news, the dogs came in and nuzzled curiously at the hospital smells on my clothes. When they satisfied themselves that the old familiar smell of me was there after all, they relaxed, curled up on the floor beside me and fell asleep. I was home.

# CHAPTER

# 10

In the next two weeks it seemed that life had gone back to normal. I taught my classes on Monday, and when my students did not run screaming from the classroom at the sight of my face, I was encouraged enough to try again on Tuesday. That worked, too, and by Wednesday, it seemed as if I'd never been away. The only lingering effects from the accident seemed to be that I tired quickly and that I was afraid to drive a car.

That first week, Peter drove me out to the auto graveyard in the North Industrial Park, and I saw the Volvo. The driver's side was mashed in, and the motor had been badly damaged. It was a write-off. As I stood looking at the car, once as familiar to me as my own face, now alien and abandoned in the snow, the man in charge of the yard came over.

"Any other car and you would have bought it, lady. I hope you know that."

I looked at him. Then I looked at my valiant Volvo. For the first time since the accident, I burst into tears.

Peter made me stop at the car dealerships on the way home and pick up some brochures.

"Therapy," he said. "You have to get back on that horse. If you're nervous about driving Sally's Porsche, get a car of your own."

But I didn't. That January I looked at a lot of brochures and went to a lot of showrooms. Somehow nothing I saw seemed quite right. By the end of the month I still hadn't driven a car.

Sally was coming back the afternoon of February first. That morning, Peter looked at me sternly when I came down to breakfast.

"The least you could do is take Sally's car around the block to make sure it turns over," he said. "It's been pretty cold. I don't think a dead battery would be much of a home-coming present for her after she was decent enough to leave you her car."

"Browbeating me into doing the brave thing, are you?" I asked.

He grinned. "Something like that. Just drive it around the corner, Mum. They came and cleaned our street this morning so it's clear sailing. You know, it really is time you got behind the wheel again."

"Okay," I said, "you win. After I take the dogs for their run, I'll drive Sally's car around the block."

"Promise?" he asked.

"Promise," I said.

When the dogs and I came up the driveway after their walk, I patted the Porsche on the hood. "Your turn now. I'll run in and get the keys and we'll go for a spin. Nothing to it."

But as I slid into the driver's seat, I was overwhelmed with anxiety. I felt frightened and clumsy. I dropped the keys on the floor, and it seemed like an omen.

When I bent down to pick them up, I saw the tuque. It was under the passenger seat, and it was dirty and wet. It looked like any of a dozen wool hats that my kids or their friends had abandoned on the car floor over the years. Except this hat didn't belong to my kids. I pulled it out and looked at it carefully. A green tuque with the logo of the Saskatoon Hilltops. Like the hat Councillor Hank Mewhort had been wearing the night of Sally's opening. But not like the one he'd been wearing at Clea Poole's funeral. That day he'd been wearing a tweed cap with ear flaps.

The hat in my hand was the tuque Sally had ripped off the head of the man who was lingering around the Porsche the night Clea was killed. I was certain of it. She must have thrown it on the seat when she drove to the gallery. In the inevitable progress of tuques in cars, it had worked its way onto the floor and out of sight.

"Out of sight, out of mind, until today," I said as I went into the kitchen and picked up the city phone book. "But, Councillor Mewhort, today your chickens have come home to roost."

The woman who answered the telephone at his office in City Hall told me I was in luck. Friday morning was the time the councillor reserved for drop-in visits from his constituents.

Half an hour later, I dropped in.

His office surprised me. I thought a man whose daily business was hand-to-hand combat with sin in Saskatoon would work in a room furnished with flaming swords and thunderbolts. Hank Mewhort's office was ordinary: a nice old oak desk, clear except for a telephone and a desk set; an empty bookshelf; a wall filled with the plaques from organizations I didn't want to know the names of, and a large and ugly ficus plant.

Councillor Mewhort was sitting at his desk. Stripped of his troops and his placards, he looked ordinary, too. He was wearing a shirt and tie and a powder-blue cardigan that had

Christmas present written all over it. His pale hair was carefully combed, and his face was pink and innocent. When he saw me he rose and held out his hand.

I didn't take it, and I didn't sit down when he motioned to the chair across from him.

"I'm a friend of Sally Love's," I said, "and I have something for you." I dropped the tuque on his empty desk, and for a moment it lay there between us, alive with possibilities.

I think I expected a scene – a denial or threats and accusations – but for the longest time there was silence as Hank Mewhort looked down at the hat.

Finally, he spoke. "You won't believe this, but I'm glad you're here. Ever since Miss Love pulled those creatures off me after the funeral, I've known I had to come forward. They had the time of Reg's death in the paper that same day, you know, 6:21. I cut the story out of the newspaper." He opened his desk drawer, pulled out the story and handed it to me. Proof of good intentions.

"Sally Love was in her house at 6:21," he said. "I could see her through the front window. She was painting. She didn't come out until later. By the time our disagreement was over, it was 6:35. I looked at the clock in my car." He looked at me steadily. His pale eyes were as guileless as a choirboy's. "I believe in doing the right thing," he said.

"Now's your chance," I said.

He walked over and took his Siwash sweater off the coat rack.

"Right," he said. "Now's my chance."

I walked to the police station on Fourth Avenue with him, and I waited with him in the reception area until Mary Ross McCourt was free to see him.

"Councillor Mewhort has information that proves Sally couldn't have killed Reg Helms," I said when Inspector McCourt came out to get us.

She raised her carefully plucked eyebrows and looked hard at him.

"True?" she asked.

"True," he said.

I watched as he followed her down the corridor and into her office. Then I sighed with relief. The wheels of justice were starting to grind.

Five hours later I was sitting at the kitchen table marking thirty-five papers on the failure of Meech Lake when the dogs started going crazy. I went to the front door and there was Sally with her arms filled with pussy willows.

I helped Sally off with her coat and took the pussy willows from her. Then we walked into the kitchen together.

"I have news," I said.

Sally smiled. "It must be pretty hot. You look like the cat that swallowed the canary."

"I feel like the cat that swallowed the canary. Sal, I found the man you had the fight with the night of the murder. And he's already been downtown and told Mary Ross McCourt his story. You're off the hook."

Sally collapsed onto the kitchen chair. "Oh, my God, Jo, this is so wonderful. I can't believe it. Is it really over? Is it really over at last?" She jumped up and hugged me. "Who was it?" she said. "Who did it turn out to be?"

"Elvis," I said. "Back from the dead to give you an alibi. Sit down and I'll tell you the whole story."

When I finished, Sally looked serious. "Who would have believed it? Councillor Hank Mewhort, the leader of the pack. Anyway, I'm in the clear. How can I ever thank you, Jo?"

"Be happy," I said. "Now let's have some coffee and talk about ordinary things. You can fill me in on Vancouver."

I made the coffee and we sat at the kitchen table in the middle of my Meech Lake papers and looked at pictures

Sally had taken of her new house in Vancouver. It was beautiful: very West Coast, surrounded by trees, lots of glass and exposed beams and dazzling views. She was filled with homeowner's pride, and as she talked she drew quick floor plans of the rooms on the cover page of one of my essays.

"Here," she said. "Here's where the door is, but we'll knock that out so Taylor can have a really spectacular bedroom. And that deck can be extended clear around the house, so you can sit there any hour of the day and feel the sun on your face. It'll be like living in a clearing in the forest." Then she stopped drawing and looked at me. "Jo, I am so happy," she said simply. Then she bent over her sketches again.

The night of February fourteenth was a Valentine itself: mild, still, moonlit, a night for lovers. It was a little after six when the taxi dropped me in front of the gallery. Everything was quiet. The invited guests wouldn't be arriving for an hour and a half. I was there early to help.

The first voice I heard that morning had been Hilda McCourt's. "Joanne, I'm taking advantage of our friendship to ask a favour. That fine young woman who's been looking after this appreciation with me just telephoned to say she has the flu. Everything is in the hands of the professionals, but as you know even professionals need a nudge now and then. Do you know Nicolas Poussin's work? Seventeenth-century French?"

"No," I said, "I don't think I do."

"Well, you should," she said. "He was the greatest of all classical painters. His motto was '*Je n'ai rien négligé*' – I overlook nothing. When it comes to this celebration of Sally Love's generosity, I think we should emulate Poussin. Come early tonight, would you, and help me keep everybody up to the mark? After all she's done for the artistic community of this city, Sally Love deserves a perfect evening."

When I saw the gallery that night, I thought of Nicolas Poussin. *"Je n'ai rien négligé"* – every detail was perfect. The bright banners bearing Sally's name were still hanging along the portico, but they were interspersed now with vertical chains of hearts, very stylized, very contemporary. In the reception area a string quartet played Ravel, and porcelain vases filled with roses perfumed the air with the sweet promise of June.

Hilda McCourt came out of the tea lounge to meet me. She had found her classic evening gown: a Chinese dress of red silk shot through with gold, form-fitting and secured from throat to ankle by elaborate frogs. She was wearing a pair of milky jade earrings that fell almost to her shoulders. When I complimented her on them, she smiled.

"They came from a friend," she said. "He was a missionary in China, but a great lover of beauty."

"I can see that," I said.

I was surprised to see her blush at the compliment, but she was quick to seize the initiative again.

"You look lovely, Joanne. Just as I predicted, your face has healed nicely, and that dress was a wise choice. Lipstick red is wonderfully vibrant on ash blondes. There's a lesson there. After forty, women should stick with true colours; pastels wash us out. Now come along. Let's get a peek at those studies that are going up for auction."

The drawings were on display in the Mendel salon. They were mounted simply, and to me at least they were a surprise. In their final form, painted in the fresco, the sexual parts had seemed spontaneous, fleshly imaginings. But here I could see the work behind the flash and the wit. The preliminary sketches showed process. Each of the genitalia was drawn in pen on a kind of grid of faint pencil lines. At the top of each page in a neat pencilled hand were notes on scale and proportion. I looked at the complex relationships of angles and circles and marvelled at the effort it must have taken for Sally to teach herself the principles of geometry she needed for her work. The studies were designated by number only.

Hilda and I went through quickly. Every so often, we'd stop at a particularly interesting one and speculate about the identity of the owner.

"Tempted to bid on any?" I asked.

"Oh, yes," she said. "Either number twenty-three or fifty-seven would add an interesting dimension to my bedroom. Now come along, we'd better check on the caterers. They've done wonders in Gallery III. If the food is as good as the ambience, we're home free."

The caterers had set up round tables throughout the room. Each table was covered by a red and white quilt of the wedding-ring pattern; in the centre a scented red candle in a hurricane lamp cast a soft glow.

I bent to look at the stitching on a quilt.

"Hand done," I said to Hilda McCourt. "It's exquisite. The whole room is exquisite."

"Here comes the man you should praise," she said as a tall, heavy-set blond man moved carefully among the tables toward us. He looked like a man who cared about the pleasures of the senses. The chain from his gold pocket watch gleamed dully against a cashmere vest the colour of claret, and his moonlike face arranged itself easily into a smile.

"Stephen Orchard," he said, "from Earthly Delights Catering."

"I've always loved your company's name," I said, "and the food, of course. It's always good news for me when I see one of your trucks parked outside a party I've been invited to."

He beamed. "Would you like a look at what you'll be eating tonight?" He picked up a stiff menu card from the table nearest us and handed it to me.

Barbecued British Columbia salmon
Consommé Madrilene
Rolled veal stuffed with watercress
Wild rice La Ronge
Fiddleheads
Tomatoes à la Provençal
Sorbet Saskatoon
Coeurs à la crème fraîche

"Perfect," I said, handing the menu back to him. Then a thought struck me. "Someone did tell you about Sally's allergies, didn't they?"

He adjusted the fold of a linen napkin. "Her husband was most conscientious. And really it's no big deal. I don't use nuts for parties this size; you'd be amazed how common that allergy is. And everything else Mr. Lachlan mentioned is simply a basis of sound cooking: organically grown ingredients, no additives, no preservatives." He smiled. "We're all growing wiser about what we put in our bodies."

"Yes," I said, "we are." I started to say more, but I felt a hand touch my elbow. I turned. It was Kyle, the gallery guard. He was wearing what must have been his dress uniform, navy blue and vaguely military.

He didn't look very cheerful. "You're not going to believe this," he said. "There are a bunch of ladies out there in ape masks."

"I believe it," I said. "They call themselves the Guerrilla Girls. They protest the way women are treated in the art world."

Kyle nodded sagely, but Hilda McCourt looked baffled. "Why would they protest an event to honour Sally?" she asked.

"She isn't exactly in tune with them philosophically," I said. "She thinks all they care about is numbers, not quality.

Sally believes that if you have talent, you'll make your way to the top. Of course, in her case that's been true."

Hilda McCourt shook her head sadly. "The solipsism of the gifted. They truly can't understand that we are not all created equal. Still, whatever Sally's philosophical differences with them might be, I don't feel we can ignore a protest by other women artists."

"If that's all it was, I'd agree," I said, "but it's more complicated than that. Sally and I got into a scuffle with this bunch after Clea Poole's funeral, and it was scary. People in masks are scary. And, Hilda, I don't think these women are interested in making a political statement. The real Guerrilla Girls, in New York, are legitimate social critics. Even Sally says they're principled. But I don't like what I've seen of these women. They frighten me. I don't like anonymity. I like to know who I'm dealing with. I don't think we owe anything to people who won't show their faces. I'd be a lot happier if they were out of here."

Hilda looked thoughtful. "We may just be giving them grist for their mill if we throw them out. I think we should see them."

"You're the boss." I shrugged and smiled at Kyle. "I guess the decision's made. We have to go see some guerrillas about a lady."

They were in the reception area, a dozen of them, wearing the outfits they had worn the day of Clea Poole's funeral: boots that came to their knees, skintight black pants, bomber jackets, big, toothy gorilla masks. Two of them were wearing gorilla hands, and the rest wore gloves. Gorillas or not, they were Canadians in an art gallery, so they were behaving themselves, waiting to deal with someone in authority.

Hilda McCourt was that somebody.

It was a compelling scene: the commanding eighty-year-old with the brilliant hair and the extravagant Chinese dress and the twelve dark figures towering over her, listening intently.

Hilda McCourt's voice was the voice of the classroom: "Why don't you tell me what you want, and I'll see how much I can accommodate you."

"We want to poster this event," one of them said, stepping forward. She handed me some of the posters she'd been holding. I looked at them quickly. They were nicely done, black and white with bold graphics. One showed a loonie with a large bite out of it; the bite represented the income lost to a Canadian artist if she happened to be a woman. Another was a list of the ten top galleries in Canada; a number beside each indicated the number of one-person exhibitions Canadian women had had at that gallery. The numbers were not impressive. Nor were the numbers on a third poster, which showed the proportion of women to men as art critics on newspapers or as directors or curators of art museums. At the bottom of each poster was the imprint: "A Public Service Message from the Guerrilla Girls: Conscience of the Art World."

I handed the posters to Hilda McCourt. "I don't see anything wrong with these," I said. "In fact, people should know this. They could put them over on that wall where the gallery's stuck all those newspaper stories about Erotobiography."

"All right," said a small figure in the back, "that's one. The next thing is we want to go to Sally's party – to represent all the women who've never had a dinner to celebrate their accomplishments."

"Or even an exhibit," said another Guerrilla Girl.

"Or even a fucking chance," said a third.

"Give us a chance," said another. "Two, four, six, eight. Empowerment now; women won't wait. Three, five, seven, nine. They've had their chance; now I want mine. Power! Now!" Their voices, muffled by the heavy masks, rose in a chorus. Their bodies began to sway rhythmically. A stocky woman at the end leaned too close to a porcelain vase filled with roses, and it fell to the floor and smashed.

Suddenly the room was silent.

"That was English soft paste porcelain, more than a hundred years old," Hilda McCourt said mildly. "A piece of great charm and vigour. Pieces like that always seem proof of our civility." She took a step toward the Guerrilla Girls. "You may certainly display your posters, but you are not welcome at this celebration. Joanne, I think we should check on the Chablis for dinner. Stephen Orchard wondered if he should bring over another case, just to be on the safe side."

I followed her across the room, but at the doorway I turned and looked back. The twelve women in the toothy masks were still standing there, staring at the broken roses and the delicate shards of blue and white and gilt. They looked like something left over from an old Ernie Kovacs TV show.

We checked the Chablis and decided that since there were three other wines being served, drinks before dinner and liqueurs afterwards, people would just have to make do. By the time we told a janitor about the broken vase and reassured Stephen Orchard, the first invited guests had arrived. Soon the gallery was filled with the scent of expensive perfumes, the rustle of evening clothes and the sounds of people laughing and calling to one another in greeting. The string quartet switched from Ravel to Cole Porter, and the evening had begun.

It seemed that everyone wore red. Nina wore a dress I remembered from the sixties, a slim, sculptured Balenciaga evening gown of velvet as lustrously red as a spring tulip. She had worn that dress to the rehearsal dinner the night before my wedding. She had been lovely then and she was lovely now. Now, as then, her dark hair was swept back, and there were pearls at her throat and earlobes. But tonight she looked worn, and I felt a pang when I thought of how little I had seen her since I'd come out of the hospital. There'd been a lot going on in my life, but obviously the past few weeks had been troubling ones for Nina, and I should have been there to help her.

Stuart wore a red tie and cummerbund with his tux. He was in an odd mood – jumpy and overly solicitous with Nina and me until Sally came in, when he walked away from us without a backward glance.

Not many people would have blamed him. In one of those ironies that revealed she was Nina's daughter after all, Sally had chosen something from the sixties, too. But where Nina had chosen a classic gown that paid homage to the timeless-ness of good design, Sally's outfit was pure costume, a sexy joke that raised a finger to people who took fashion seriously. She was wearing a one-piece jumpsuit, white lace appliquéd on some sort of stretchy net with matching leggings. There wasn't much lace in the jumpsuit, but there was a lot of net and a lot of Sally. Later she told me her outfit was a Rudi Gernreich, and I smiled at the memories of see-through blouses, topless bathing suits and promises of revolution.

From the moment she came in, Stuart was all over Sally – leaving his arm around her shoulders after the initial greeting, bending his face close to hers when she talked, stroking her hair with his hand. Finally, laughing, she shook him off, the way a woman shakes off a drunk at a party. But Stuart Lachlan wasn't drunk, and he wouldn't be shaken off. When Sally started in the direction of the bar, he followed her, still trying somehow to get his hands on her. It was as if he was afraid to leave her alone. Nina and I watched the scene in silence.

"Whatever do you make of that display, Ni?" I asked. But she didn't answer; she just watched the space where they had been with an expression I couldn't fathom.

And then there was another tableau. Kyle, the gallery guard, had approached Izaak Levin. They were across the room, and I couldn't hear their conversation, but when Izaak limped toward us, Kyle watched him thoughtfully.

When Izaak Levin joined us, I was amazed at the change in him. I hadn't seen him since the day of the accident, five weeks ago, but he looked twenty years older. He skin had a greyish cast and he seemed distinctly unwell. Selling his integrity was apparently taking its toll. We had just started talking when an old friend from the political days came over, full of excitement, to introduce me to her new husband. By the time I turned back to Izaak, he and Nina had moved to the side of the room. He was whispering something in her ear and he had his hand on her arm. When finally he walked away, Nina scrubbed at the place where his hand had rested as if she had been touched by something loathsome.

Loathsome or not, when it came time for dinner, Izaak Levin was seated at Sally's right, and on his right was Nina. I was at their table, and we were an uncomfortable grouping. Stuart was on Sally's left, and I was beside him. Next to me was Hugh Rankin-Carter, the art critic. On his left was Hilda McCourt. She'd positioned herself beside the only person I'd never met at our table, a woman named Annie Christensen, who had parlayed a smart marriage and a genius for mathematics into a substantial fortune. She was known as a generous supporter of the arts, and it was no accident that, boy-girl seating be damned, Hilda had put her at the table with the star of the evening.

The meal was magnificent, but dinner was not a pleasant affair. Hugh Rankin-Carter was a man with real power in the art world, and Annie Christensen was a philanthropist with deep pockets; the fact that both were seated at our table was apparently too much for Izaak and Stu. A tense rivalry, part professional, part sexual, seemed to spring up between them.

Whatever his faults, Izaak Levin had always been a witty and self-effacing man, but that night he told pointless repetitive stories whose sole purpose seemed to be to lament the brilliant career he'd given up for Sally and to celebrate his influence on her art. Not to be outdone, Stu quoted long passages of analysis from his book.

Sally sat between them looking trapped and miserable. She was patient longer than I would have thought possible, but finally she turned on Stu. At first she kept her voice low.

"Okay, Stu, that's enough. You're boring the tits off everybody. Now be still, and listen to me for a minute. You might actually learn something. No matter what that ridiculous book of yours says, I'm not some sort of holy innocent the great god of art drips paint through. I actually know what I'm doing." Her voice rose with anger. "I told you last night I can't believe you could have lived with me five years without understanding one single thing about what I do. Damn it, Stu, if I could put what I see into words, why would I paint it?" She shook her head in exasperation, and when she spoke again, her voice was weary. "Look, the best thing to do with that book is junk it. If it doesn't come out, nobody will be the wiser, but if you actually let that stuff get published, everybody is going to know you're . . ."

"Dumb as shit." Hugh Rankin-Carter smiled as he finished the sentence for her.

Izaak Levin poured himself a glass of wine and laughed. "Not bad, Hughie," he said.

Sally looked at him with anger. "You're no better, Izaak. All that whining about how you sacrificed your career for mine. Tell me, when was the last time you earned a dime that wasn't connected to me?"

In one of those terrible moments that happen at parties, the room was suddenly quiet, and Sally's words, bell clear, hung in the air.

Izaak's face sagged. Across the table, I was surprised to see a flicker of pleasure cross Nina Love's face.

A woman I recognized from Clea's funeral had been moving from group to group taking pictures. She came over to our table.

"Not now, Anya," Sally said, but the woman kept snapping away until Sally flared and told her to get lost.

The rolled veal arrived, savoury and tender enough to cut with a fork, but the misery continued at our table. Stuart sat silent, his face a mask carved by humiliation. Izaak Levin drifted into the self-pitying phase of drunkenness, talking incoherently about how Sally could never begin to understand all the things he had done to protect her. Finally, he lurched off to the men's room. When he came back, his fly was undone and Sally, with a savage look, bent over and zipped him up.

"It's over, Izaak. No use advertising any more."

In my two brief encounters with him, Hugh Rankin-Carter had struck me more as gadfly than peacemaker, but the crosscurrents at our table became so menacing that even he tried to pour oil on the troubled waters. After Sally's outburst, Hugh leaned across to Nina and asked her to tell him about the early fifties when Des Love had scandalized Toronto the Good with his bold and sensual paintings.

Nina was a gifted storyteller but that night she told one story remotely and badly, and when Sally corrected her on a detail, Nina excused herself and left the table. As she moved behind Sally's chair, a flashbulb went off in her face, and I saw her freeze as if she'd been shot.

Only Hilda McCourt and Annie Christensen seemed immune to the tensions. They ate with gusto and chatted happily about art and theatre. I envied them, and I was relieved when the table was cleared and the only course left was dessert. Stephen Orchard was known for the dramatic presentation of dessert at the parties he catered.

Certainly, no one in the room that night would ever forget the arrival of his coeurs à la crème fraîche. The lights were extinguished, leaving the room illuminated only by the candles blazing in hurricane lamps at the centre of each table. The string quartet struck up "My Funny Valentine," and a half-dozen red heart-shaped spotlights focused on the entrance to the tea salon. Through the door came a procession of waiters carrying silver trays. As the waiters moved to the tables, the spotlights swept the room. It was a knockout.

Our waiter swooped dramatically in front of Sally, picked up the first dessert and began to serve. There were eight glass plates on the tray; at the centre of each plate was a creamy heart surrounded by strawberry sauce. When we all had one, Hugh Rankin-Carter leaned across to me.

"Tacky but effective," he said.

It happened just at that moment. The spotlights were turned off, but in the darkness we could see figures running. They moved quickly, blowing out the candles that were the only light in the room. Soon the room was in total darkness, but not before everyone in it had had a good look at the Guerrilla Girls in action.

Afterwards, we learned that most people thought they were part of the entertainment. Whatever the explanation, no one was particularly upset. For a few seconds there was nervous laughter, then people lit the candles at their tables, and it was over.

Except it wasn't over. The Guerrilla Girls had left a large red envelope on each table, and you could hear the intake of breath around the room as people opened them. Sally ripped open ours, looked quickly at the poster that was inside, then handed it to me. She looked shaken but defiant.

"Jo, we should have pounded them into the ground when we had the chance."

I looked at the poster. It was black and white, like the others, but this one had an illustration, a blowup of what must have been a police photo of Clea Poole the night she was murdered. She was naked, lying face down on the barbed wire bridal bed. Underneath in heavy black letters were the words, "Remembering a martyr to women's art on Valentine's Day."

I shuddered, but I tried to match Sally's tone. "There'll be other chances," I said.

Hugh Rankin-Carter took the poster by two fingers, shook his head in disgust and dropped it in a leather bag that was the twin of the one he'd given Sally the night of the opening.

"Pathetic," he said. "But if they want recognition, I'll write a column about them. And I'll be sure to mention that the one who reached in front of me has apparently taken a philosophical stand against deodorant." He turned to Sally. "Don't let them ruin your party, Sal. My grandfather always said, 'Life is uncertain, eat dessert first.' Now, be a good girl and eat your coeur before it melts."

Sally grinned at him and stuck her spoon into the centre of her perfect heart. She swallowed the first bite, then waved her spoon at Hugh.

"Yum," she said.

She was right. I began eating my dessert and listening to the conversation between Hilda McCourt and Annie Christensen. I don't know when I knew something was wrong. At some point, I looked over and saw that Sally had pushed her chair back from the table. There was an odd stricken look on her face. Then she reached down as if she were searching for something on the floor. When she sat up, her eyes were wide with fear. She braced herself against the table as if she were afraid of falling.

I started toward her.

"Sal?" I said.

"I need my bag," she said. "I'm having a reaction to something in the food."

I dived under the table. It was hard to see in the darkness. Stu was already under there raking the floor with his hands. Sally's purse wasn't there.

"Somebody get a doctor," I said, and I went over to Sally. She was slumped in her chair, and her breathing was laboured. She looked at me in terror.

"I can't get air in," she said.

I stroked her cheek. "It'll be all right," I said. "They're getting a doctor."

The gallery had set up a microphone for people to make thank-you speeches at the end of dinner, and as if on cue, I heard the soft American voice of Hugh Rankin-Carter asking if there was a doctor in the house.

There were seven medical doctors in the room that night: three urologists, the plastic surgeon who had sewn my face up after the accident, a proctologist and two psychiatrists. A few drops of epinephrine would have saved Sally's life, but there was no epinephrine in that room. Sally's evening bag with the emergency supply she always carried with her had disappeared, and none of the doctors had come to the party prepared to meet death. I could hear one of them calling for an ambulance; she was very specific in her instructions about the epinephrine, but it didn't matter, because by the time the ambulance attendants ran into the room, Sally was dead.

She died slowly and in mortal terror. She deserved better.

Izaak Levin was luckier. His death was quick. When the ambulance attendants began loading Sally's body on their stretcher, Izaak made a little crying sound and fell to the floor. The doctors tried CPR. They struggled over him for what seemed to me to be a painfully long time, but nothing worked.

"Heart," one of the doctors said laconically as he stood up and turned away from Izaak's body. "He just wasn't salvageable."

Ours was the last table the police let go. The people at our table were interviewed separately and then together, but the police seemed less interested in our relationship with Sally than in the Guerrilla Girls, and we were questioned again and again about the sequence of events that began with the second dousing of the lights and the entrance of the Guerrilla Girls and ended with Sally's death. Finally, they told us we were free to leave.

It was one-thirty in the morning. Mary Ross McCourt offered to take her aunt home, and Hilda followed her gratefully. It was the first time I had ever seen her appear old and helpless. Annie Christensen and Hugh Rankin-Carter left together. They were staying at the same hotel, and as they left I heard Annie invite Hugh to join her in the bar for a nightcap. No one wanted to be alone.

When the police gave us permission to go, I walked over and put my arms around Nina. She held tight to me, and then she looked at me hard.

"You're all the daughter I have now," she said.

People, including me, laugh at the phrase, "I thought my heart would break," but that night as I looked into Nina's eyes, I knew it could happen. When she kissed my cheek, I could smell the familiar scent of Joy. Always that perfume had meant I was safe, home free. That night, the magic didn't seem to work. As I watched Nina take Stuart Lachlan's arm and lead him gently out of the room, I knew that none of us would ever be safe again.

I couldn't leave the room without looking around one last time. The police hadn't let the people from Stephen Orchard's catering company clear the tables. The candles had, of course, guttered and burned out long ago, but the coeurs à la crème fraîche were still there, and that is my last memory of that night: three hundred creamy hearts dissolving into red.

# CHAPTER

# 11

It was a little after 2:00 a.m. when Peter and I pulled into the driveway on Osler Street. As soon as the police told me I could go, I'd called home. Pete had answered on the first ring. Every light in our house was blazing. It wasn't a night for shadows or dark corners. Mieka and Greg were waiting for me at the front door; Angus was in his room with the dogs. As soon as he heard my voice, Angus came running down the hall. He threw his arms around me and buried his face in my neck.

"This really sucks," he said. "This really, really sucks."

I tried to think of something I could say that would make it better, but there wasn't anything. I pulled him close, and we walked into the living room together. When I sat down on the couch, Angus curled up against me the way he used to when he was little. We were both shivering. Mieka came in with an afghan and covered us both.

The afghan was the one Sally had pulled around her the night Clea Poole died. A flash of memory. Sally in a rare moment of doubt, seeking reassurance. "Do you think Taylor will ever make one of these for her notorious mother?" And me, reassuring, "Sure, notorious mothers are the best kind."

Mieka and Greg stayed at the house that night. It was nice of them, but it didn't make any difference. Every time I closed my eyes I saw Sally as she had been in those last seconds, her lovely face frozen in the primal panic of an animal at the moment of death. Anything was better than that. I went downstairs and sat in the chair by the window in my dark living room. Across the street I could see the familiar shapes of the neighbours' houses. I looked at them and thought about nothing. When the sky began to lighten and the first cars started to drive along the street, I went into the kitchen and made coffee. I poured myself a cup, but somehow the mug slipped from my hand. It clattered noisily across the floor, leaving a dark spoor in its wake. I picked up a cloth, but when I knelt to clean up the mess, I started to sob. I started, and I couldn't stop. Barefoot, shivering in my thin cotton nightie, I sat on the kitchen floor and cried until I felt an arm around my shoulders, and my daughter led me upstairs to bed. She stayed with me till I fell asleep.

I didn't sleep long, but when I woke up I felt better. I showered and pulled on jeans and a sweatshirt. When I went downstairs, the kids were sitting around the kitchen table and Mieka was making French toast.

"Your favourite," she said, "so you have to have some."

"I will, later," I said. "Honestly. Right now all I want is some coffee."

I'd just taken a sip when the phone rang. Mieka answered it, then turned to me.

"For you. Shall I ask him to call back?"

I shook my head and took the receiver. It was Hugh Rankin-Carter.

"Joanne, I've found out some things I'd rather you heard from me than . . . well, than from others. Would you like to meet me somewhere? Or I could come there if it's better for you."

"Why don't you come here?" I said. "My daughter's just making French toast. If you haven't already had breakfast, you could eat with us."

"I'll be there as soon as I can get a cab," he said.

He was at our front door in fifteen minutes. As I helped him off with his coat, I noticed that he had shaved and was wearing a fresh shirt. He still looked like hell. I caught a glimpse of my face in the hall mirror. I looked like hell, too.

We went into the kitchen and I introduced the kids to Hugh. The boys said hello and excused themselves. Peter had a class. Angus asked if he could go back to bed. It seemed as good a thing to do as any. When they left, Mieka turned to us.

"Two orders of French toast?" she asked.

"Sounds delightful," Hugh said.

"Nothing for me," I said.

"You have to eat," Hugh said curtly. He smiled at Mieka. "I'll bet Joanne can be tempted." He turned to me. "Didn't your mother ever tell you about keeping your strength up in a crisis?"

"My mother limited herself to telling me I'd ruined her life."

He raised his eyebrows. "Ah, the search for the mother. That explains Nina. Sally was always baffled at how close you and her mother were."

"They were very different women," I said. "I don't think they were ever very fair in their assessments of each other."

"From what I've seen of Nina Love, Sally was more than fair," Hugh said. He sipped his coffee. "Joanne, about last night. I'm afraid I have something in the nature of a revelation. After I had my drink with Annie Christensen, I went down to the police station. The boys and girls in blue were amazingly forthcoming. You'd be touched to see how people welcome me when I tell them I'm from a Toronto newspaper. Anyway, the first thing I learned is of forensic interest. Sally died of food-induced anaphylactic reaction. Her coeur à la crème fraîche was covered in powdered almonds."

I felt my throat start to close. "Stephen Orchard knew she couldn't eat almonds," I said weakly.

"Stephen Orchard didn't put them there, Joanne. The police found a little plastic bag in the pocket of the jacket Izaak Levin was wearing when he died. It had been emptied, but there were traces of something that the police, with their flair for language, are at the moment calling 'potential almond residue.'"

I picked up my coffee cup, but my hands were shaking so badly I could barely get it to my lips.

"There's more," Hugh said. "They found Sally's purse with the epinephrine kit. It was in the gallery cloakroom. Jo, the purse was in the pocket of Izaak Levin's overcoat."

"So he killed her," I said.

"It looks that way," said Hugh. "Either that or, after all his rude comments about my lifestyle, old Izaak's turned out to be a cross-dresser."

Despite everything, I laughed.

Mieka brought over two plates of French toast. "I'll leave you two alone now. Shout if you need me."

"Thanks," I said. "For everything." I took a bite of French toast. "Good," I said. "It really is. You were right about eating, Hugh."

He smiled and put maple syrup on his French toast. "So what do you think?"

"I don't know," I said. "I don't know if I even care. All those questions last night about the Guerrilla Girls. I guess they're off the hook now."

"I don't think they're off the hook at all," Hugh said. "I'm a visual arts editor, not a crime reporter, but I had the distinct impression last night that the police aren't fond of coincidence. You know, Jo, the Guerrilla Girls did turn out the lights, and they were running around that room. Who knows what they did in the dark. They could have been working with Izaak Levin."

"Yes," I agreed, "they could have been working with him, or it could have been the other way round."

Hugh went over, picked up the coffeepot and filled our cups. "You've lost me," he said.

"I guess it's possible," I said, "that the Guerrilla Girls could have set Izaak Levin up. You know, Hugh, in all the confusion after the lights went out it wouldn't have been hard to slip something as small as an empty plastic baggie into a jacket pocket. The Guerrilla Girl who came to our table was standing right between Izaak and Nina. I remember that clearly. And it certainly would have been easy for her to grab Sally's purse. It was slung over the back of her chair all evening. You must have noticed it – one of those antique evening bags with a chain so you can carry it over your shoulder."

Suddenly I was so weary I could barely move. "Why are we doing this?" I asked. "It doesn't matter. It doesn't change anything. We can sit here till doomsday and nothing we figure out is going to change the past twenty-four hours."

Hugh looked as weary as I felt. He stood up. "I think it's time to go," he said.

He called a cab, and when it came, I walked him to the front door.

"Take care of yourself," he said. "Thank your daughter for the breakfast."

"Come back again," I said.

"Every time I'm in Saskatoon." Then he smiled. "Be sure to wear that shirt next time. It's a little Dolly Parton but very cute. I'll bet your kids got it for you."

I didn't remember what I was wearing. I looked down: bubble-gum pink with sequins saying *I LOVE JO*. I leaned forward and kissed his cheek.

"You lose your bet," I said. "It wasn't from my kids. It was a present from a friend."

It didn't take me long to decide to go to Nina's. I was exhausted, but I couldn't get clear of what she had said to me the night before. "You're all the daughter I have now." It was my duty to tell her about Izaak Levin. As strained as her relationship with Sally had been, this would be a shock. I had to be there to help her deal with it.

I went up and changed into my best black skirt and sweater and called a cab. All the way to Spadina Crescent, the cab driver kept up a running commentary on Sally's murder. I couldn't seem to work up the energy to tell him to stop. Traffic near the gallery was heavy. The prospect of seeing the building where four shocking deaths had occurred really brought out the citizens. Apparently, Stuart Lachlan's address was still secret because the only cars in front of number seventeen were Stu's matched Mercedes. The family of snow people had been revised a little by thaws and storms but they were still perky. A banner, white with big red letters and a border of hearts, stretched from the father to the daughter. HAPPY VALENTINE'S FROM TAYLOR LOVE LACHLAN, it said.

I took a deep breath before I lifted the brass door knocker. Nina answered the door. She was wearing a white cashmere dress that I didn't remember, very chic, very flattering. An antique gold locket gleamed at her neck, and in her ears were tiny hoops of chased gold. She took both my hands in hers and pulled me gently inside.

"I'm so glad it's you, Jo," she said in her low breathy voice. "I need help and I was debating with myself about whether it was too early to call you."

"It could never be too early, Ni," I said.

She helped me off with my coat and then, hand in hand, we walked into the living room.

I don't know what I expected. Neither Nina nor Stuart Lachlan was the keening or rending garments type, but everything was so serene, so life as usual. Mozart was on the CD player; there were bowls of shaggy white chrysanthemums on the mantel and coffee table, and the air smelled of coffee and fresh baking.

I turned to Nina. "You know I'd do anything for you, Ni, but it certainly looks as if everything's in hand."

"Looks can be deceiving," she said. She made a sweeping gesture toward the Chinese Chippendale desk. "Really, I've just begun."

I looked over at the desk. There was an open telephone book on it and a notepad with notations in Nina's neat backhand.

"I'm just trying to think of everything that needs to be done and match up the chore list with the names of the local people. I don't know this city well enough to make an informed decision myself, but I thought I could make some preliminary lists for Stuart to choose from. This is going to be a trying day for him."

"For all of us," I said.

"Of course," she agreed. "We're all the walking wounded today."

"Ni, I have more news. Could we sit down?"

She drew me over to the couch. "I'm sorry, Jo. You'll have to forgive me. It's just that there's so much . . ."

"I'm afraid I'm going to add to it, dear. The police have completed some of their investigation, and they have some

ideas about what might have happened last night." I moved
closer to her and told her about Izaak and the almonds and the
epinephrine. She listened with her back ramrod straight and
her hands cupping one another loosely, like a woman waiting
to have her photograph taken. Her calm unnerved me.

"Nina, did you understand what I said? The police think
Izaak was the one."

"Yes," she said, "I heard you."

In the kitchen there was the treble pinging sound of an
oven timer. Nina stood up and gave me a shaky smile.

"Currant scones," she said, "Stuart's favourite. I'm going
to fix a tray for him and take it upstairs. I'll bring us something, too, Jo. Please, just be patient and make yourself comfortable."

It was a tall order. I walked over to Nina's desk. The telephone book was open to funeral homes. I shuddered and
walked through the dining room to the bay window that
overlooked the backyard. Nina's evening dress, tulip red, and
Stu's tuxedo were out there, hanging side by side on the
clothesline. Even before smoking had become the great
social sin, Nina had hated the lingering smell of cigarettes.
She always hung her clothes out to air after she had been
somewhere where people smoked. There had been smoking
last night. And there had been murder.

For a while, my mind drifted. White think. Then I felt
someone beside me. I looked down and Taylor Love Lachlan
was there. Her blond hair was smoothed back behind an
*Alice in Wonderland* black velvet bow, and she was wearing
a Black Watch tartan skirt and a white blouse. She was
silent, intent on what she saw through the window.

"Look," she said finally, "when the wind blows, Nina's
dress and Daddy's suit look like they're dancing on the
clothesline."

I smiled and gave her shoulder a squeeze.

"Sally died, you know," she said conversationally. "I was asleep, but when I woke up, Daddy told me Sally had gone to heaven."

I didn't know what to say. I stood there, numb, looking into the yard, my hand resting on Taylor's shoulder. The wind had picked up, and Taylor was right. Nina's dress and Stu's tuxedo looked as if they were dancing. Inexplicably, I felt a clutch of panic.

But suddenly behind me there was Nina's voice, warm, reassuring. "Come and eat something, you two." And I felt safe again. She was sitting at the dining-room table in a pose I'd seen a thousand times: a tray set with the thinnest cups, a teapot, plates, linen napkins, something still warm from the oven for tea.

Izaak Levin was not mentioned again that morning. As Nina talked quietly about the kinds of birds that would come to their bird feeder when the great migrations north began, I saw that she was trying to protect Taylor and Stuart by enclosing them in a world of familiar pleasures. There was no place for Sally's murderer at that table, and so we talked of birds and gardens and Stuart's summer home at Stay Away Lake, a hundred miles north of the city. Stuart wanted to go there after everything was settled, Nina said in her soft voice. He loved the house at Stay Away Lake. His family had owned it since before he was born, and everything was exactly as it had been half a century ago.

"He needs that now," said Nina. "So much has changed."

"So much has changed." I repeated those words to myself as I started the long walk to Osler Street. I didn't even make it to the bridge before the tears started. I didn't care. I stood and looked down at the river and cried. When I was finished, I took a deep breath, squared my shoulders and started to walk again. The sky was overcast but the air was fresh, and when I turned up the back alley toward our house, I was feeling in control. My neighbour was out in her backyard taking sheets off the line. The sheets were frozen, and she had to wrestle with them to get them folded and in her laundry hamper. I thought of Nina's evening dress and Stuart's tuxedo dancing against the grey February sky. And then out of nowhere, a poem, something we used to write in autograph books when I was in grade school:

> I love you. I love you. I love you almighty.
> I wish your pyjamas were next to my nightie.
> Now don't get excited.
> Now don't lose your head.
> I mean on the clothesline and not in the bed.

When I walked across our backyard, I couldn't tell if I was laughing or crying.

Angus was sitting in the den watching a kids' show that he'd outgrown years ago. He was wearing a T-shirt he'd bought himself at the joke shop in the mall. On the front a cartoon rooster with a huge beak and a macho leer was strutting on a beach filled with hens; underneath it said, "Chicks Dig Big Peckers."

I gestured toward the TV. "Anything new in Mr. Dressup's world?"

"Nope, everything's just the same." Then he looked up at me. I could see he'd been crying, but he tried a smile. "Nothing ever changes on Mr. Dressup. You know that, Mum. That's why I'm watching."

At three o'clock I went over and gave my senior class a reading assignment. There was a message on my desk to call Izaak Levin. I shuddered when I noticed the message was dated the day before.

When I got home, Angus met me at the door. "I'm going down to the Y to shoot baskets with James if it's okay."

"It's okay," I said. "Supper's at five-thirty."

"What are we having?"

"Takeout, your choice."

"Fish and chips?"

"Sounds good to me," I said. "I could use a load of grease right now."

He smiled. "Right. Oh, I almost forgot, Sally's mother came over with some flowers," he said. "They're in the living room."

On the coffee table was the Japanese porcelain bowl with the painted swimming fish. Serene. Beautiful. Nina had filled it with white anemone, and there was a note card with a line written in her neat backhand propped up against it. "Remembering and cherishing, N."

I sighed and went to the phone. She answered on the first ring, and when she heard my voice, her relief was evident.

"Jo, thank heavens it's you. I'm feeling very alone right now. Stuart's been drinking all day. He's so withdrawn I can't reach him. And I think the reality of her mother's death is starting to hit Taylor. She's just clinging to me. I haven't been able to get anything done. You said this morning that if there was anything you could do, I should ask. Well, I'm asking."

"I'm here," I said.

"Someone needs to go to the funeral home and make some decisions. And a curious thing. A priest came to the house this afternoon. He said Sally was a parishioner of his. That's a surprise, at least to me. At any rate, he'll do the funeral, but he needs to talk to someone from the family." Her voice broke. "Jo, there is no one from the family. I'm all alone."

"I'll go, Nina," I said. "Just give me the names and addresses."

"Thank you, Jo. I knew I could count on you."

When I hung up the phone, I felt about as wretched as I could remember. I put my face in my hands and leaned against the telephone table. After a while, I felt a tap on my shoulder. I looked up. Peter was standing there.

"I have to go and pick out the coffin," I said.

"You'll need a ride," he said simply.

I was glad I had him with me. The people at the funeral home were kind and helpful, but making funeral arrangements was a lousy job. After we finished, Pete dropped me off at St. Thomas More Chapel.

I had called Father Gary Ariano before dinner and told him I'd meet him at eight o'clock. The college bells were chiming when I walked in the front door, and Father Ariano was waiting for me. He was a dark-haired, athletic man in early middle age, very intense. He was wearing blue jeans and a sweatshirt from Loyola University. He held out his hand in greeting, and I followed him up two flights of stairs through a door marked "Private" into the priests' common room. It was a comfortable room, with an outsize aquarium, a wall of windows that looked out onto the campus and a generously stocked bar.

"What'll it be?" asked Father Ariano.

"Bourbon, please, and ice."

Father Ariano opened a Blue for himself and poured a generous splash of Old Grand-Dad over ice for me. We sat down on a couch in front of the windows. It was a foggy night, and below us the lights of the campus glowed, otherworldly.

I didn't know where to begin but after we'd had a few minutes to grow easy with one another, Father Ariano began for me.

"Sally told me once that the only good things about the Catholic church were its art collection and its funerals."

"And yet she was a regular communicant?" I asked.

"She was," he said. "She came most often on weekdays. There's a mass around five, and sometimes we'd go out for a sandwich after or she'd come up here and we'd talk."

"It's hard to think of Sally as devout," I said.

"I think Sally would have called herself interested rather than devout. The nature of faith and the faithful interested her. She was a very bright woman."

"Not just a holy innocent the great god of art dripped paint through," I said.

He smiled. "That sounds like a direct quote from our friend Sally. People always underestimated her. Stuart Lachlan certainly did. He put her in a terrible position when he wrote that book. It was an incredible breach of trust."

"Not the first in her life," I said.

He looked at me oddly. "No," he said, "not the first and not the only. But don't get me started on that. Look, I guess we'd better discuss the details for the funeral."

"Right," I said.

Father Ariano was, as they say, a godsend: factual, presenting options, suggesting choices. When we'd finished, I stood up.

"Thanks," I said. "I guess that's it."

Father Ariano looked at me. "Except for one thing."

I waited.

He squeezed his right hand together, crushing his beer can. "Except," he said, "that this is the shits. It really is the shits."

"That's what my son said, too."

"Smart kid," he said, standing. "Come on, follow me, I'll show you the chapel."

We went down the stairs to the main floor, but instead of going toward the front doors, we turned down a wide and brightly lit hall. On one side were pictures of the priests who had been heads of the order. On the other were clothing racks, the kind you see in department stores. Arranged on each rack, seemingly by ecclesiastical season and size, were dozens of clerical vestments.

"This is where we robe," Father Ariano said casually, "and here," he said, as we walked through some double doors, "is where we go to work."

The air in the chapel was cool and smelled of candle wax, furniture polish and, lingeringly, of wet wool. The chapel was uncluttered and attractive: white painted walls and plain blond pews arranged in a semicircle to face the gleaming wooden cross suspended from the ceiling above the altar. It looked like any of a dozen chapels I'd seen that were designed for the university community at worship. But on the north wall was a mural, and it was to the mural that Gary Ariano directed my attention when we came through the doors.

"There's our prize," he said.

From a distance the mural was conventionally pretty: a prairie field on a summer's day with Christ at the centre performing the miracle of the loaves and fishes. I wasn't much interested.

"The colours are lovely," I said dismissively.

Gary Ariano said, "Go closer. Get a good look."

Up close, the mural glowed with apocalyptic light. Dark storm clouds in the corner menaced the perfect blue of the sky; under the crowds that circled the field where Jesus stood, the earth was cracking open, and arms shaking their fists at God thrust themselves through wounds in the earth.

"That just about reflects my world view at the moment," I said.

"I knew you'd like it," said Gary Ariano dryly, as we turned and walked out of the chapel and back into the world.

# CHAPTER

# 12

Sally's funeral was set for Monday afternoon, the first day of the university's February break. The administration had introduced the break a quarter of a century before because the university had the highest suicide rate in the country. The students still called it Dead Week. The period between Friday night when I walked home through the darkness from my meeting with Father Gary Ariano to the morning of the funeral was a blur for me: arranging for musicians, choosing the proper spray of flowers for the coffin, the right arrangements for the tall copper vases the college chapel provided, talking to Mieka about food for the reception afterwards – busywork, but anything beat thinking about Sally.

And anything was better than thinking about Izaak Levin. I couldn't get my mind around the fact that the brilliant man Sally and I had dreamed over that hot, starry summer was a killer. Looking at my reflection in the hall mirror, I saw the same woman I always saw, but I felt like Saint Bartholomew, flayed alive. In desperation, I grabbed my gym bag and went to Maggie's. The aerobics class was in the same gym Sally and I had been in before Christmas, and she was everywhere in that room for me, face set in concentration, body slick with sweat, invulnerable. Halfway through the workout, I couldn't take the memories any more, and I ran to the dressing room and wept.

I talked to Nina many times that weekend but I saw her only once, when Mieka and I went Saturday morning to take Taylor shopping for an outfit she could wear to the services on Monday.

We pulled up in front of the Lachlans' at nine o'clock. Stuart met us at the door. He looked, as the Irish say, like a man who has spent the night asleep in his own grave, but he helped Taylor on with her coat and walked us out to the road.

When he saw Mieka waiting in her car, Stu looked at me. "Haven't you replaced your car yet, Joanne?"

I shook my head. "No," I said, "there doesn't seem to have been any time."

Stu fumbled in his pocket and produced a set of keys. "Here," he said, pointing to the two silvery Mercedes in his driveway. "Take one of them. I'm not going anywhere, and even Nina can't drive them both at once. Jo, she told me you're handling everything for us. Keep the car as long as you want. Keep it forever."

Taylor had already climbed into the front seat of Stuart's car, so I went to tell Mieka I didn't need a ride after all. When I slid into the driver's seat, I smiled at Taylor.

"Okay, miss, let's go look at some dresses." It wasn't until I pulled into a parking place at the mall that it hit me. For the first time since the accident, I had driven a car again.

I was still driving the Mercedes when I pulled up in front of St. Thomas More Chapel an hour before Sally's funeral. I'd come early because I wanted to make sure everything was perfect.

As I walked into the hushed coolness of the chapel it seemed as if everything was as it should be. A screen was in

place to the side of the altar. Hugh Rankin-Carter was giving
the eulogy, and he wanted to show some of Sally's work as
he talked about her life. The college's copper urns had been
replaced by two of Nina's most beautiful lacquerware water
jars, and they were filled with orchids. The mass cards with
the reproduction of *Perfect Circles*, Sally's painting of us that
last summer at the lake, were piled neatly on a table by the
door. "*Je n'ai rien négligé.*" Me and Nicolas Poussin.

During the funeral, my children and I sat under the mural
of the prairie Jesus performing the miracle of the loaves and
fishes. He was wearing a white robe, and His arm was raised
in benediction. I tried to keep my eyes on that sign of bless-
ing, but I kept seeing other things: Taylor, looking like a
Parisian schoolgirl in her black double-breasted coat and
beret, pulling back from her father and grandmother as they
walked up the centre aisle. Stuart stumbling and Nina reaching to steady him as they took their places in the front pew.
Hugh Rankin-Carter at the lectern, unrecognizable for a
moment in a dark business suit, his face broken by anguish.
Hilda McCourt, back ramrod straight, saying good-bye to
another free spirit. And in front of the altar, inescapable, the
plain pine box that held all that was left of Sally's grace and
laughter and beauty.

We had taken two cars to the chapel. Taylor was going to
our house with my kids right after the funeral. She said she
didn't want to see them put Sally under the snow. I didn't,
either, but I was an adult; I didn't have any options.

As I drove to the cemetery, I was glad to be alone. Nina
had asked me to ride with them, but at the funeral Stuart
had broken down completely, and I knew if I had to spend
any time with him, I'd go over the edge, too.

Prospect Cemetery was on the river south of the city. The
road into it was narrow, overgrown with bushes. In the

summer the bushes became a dense and primitive place where city kids would drink beer and make love. But as I looked at that windswept hill, bleak as a moor, it was impossible to believe in a world of pleasure and hot coupling.

There were only a handful of us at the graveside: Father Ariano, Nina, Stuart, Hugh Rankin-Carter, Hilda McCourt and me. I didn't react when they lowered Sally's casket into the ground. I think by then I had entered a place in my mind that was beyond reaction.

Nina had invited me to come back to their house for a drink. As I pulled onto Spadina Crescent, I wondered if I should have been so quick to say I'd come. I didn't remember the drive from the cemetery at all, and when I looked at the art gallery I felt a stab of panic. It seemed unfamiliar, changed from the place I knew. Disoriented and frightened, I tried to grasp what was different, and then suddenly I knew.

The banners were gone. They had taken down the yellow banners that had celebrated Sally's name against the winter sky since the week before Christmas. In one of her books, Virginia Woolf says something about how we experience the death of someone we love not at their funeral but when we come upon a pair of their old shoes. I hadn't come upon Sally's old shoes in the portico of the gallery, but for emotional impact, the missing banners were close enough. I pulled into the parking lot, put my head on the steering wheel and wept.

On the dashboard in front of me was the mass card from Sally's funeral. Hugh Rankin-Carter had chosen the epigraph. It was from Jacques Lipchitz, the great sculptor. "All my life as an artist I have asked myself: what pushes me continually to make art. The answer is simple. Art is our unique way of fighting death and achieving immortality. And in this continuity of art, of creation and denial of death, we find God."

Tuesday morning was Izaak Levin's memorial service. I wore the same black wool suit I had worn the day before to Sally's funeral. Dead Week.

Izaak's service was at a small performance studio in the old fine arts building. Whoever had chosen the venue had made a wise choice. Not many people came to say good-bye to a man who was alleged to have killed four people. That morning as I had rummaged through my dresser for a pair of black panty hose, I had come up with a dozen reasons I shouldn't go.

A dozen reasons not to, and just one that compelled me to go, but it overrode all the rest. I was there for Sally. I had a sense that she wanted me there, and so I was there.

Someone had taken pains with Izaak Levin's memorial service. There was a good jazz quartet playing fifties progressive jazz: "Round Midnight," "Joyspring" and some tunes I recognized from the album *Kind of Blue* by Miles Davis. Between numbers, three men who looked like contemporaries of Izaak's read from his art criticism.

There was no coffin. Izaak Levin had been cremated as soon as the coroner released his body.

I didn't know any of the people in that room, but one woman held my attention, mostly, I think, because she seemed like such an unlikely mourner. She was a small, square woman in her sixties, nicely but not fashionably dressed in a royal blue crepe dress. Her jet-black hair was upswept, and her face still had traces of plump prettiness. When the service was over, she shook hands with the musicians and the men who had read. Then she turned and walked toward me.

As she held out her hand, she smiled.

"I'm Ellie Levin, Izaak's sister, and I wanted to thank you for coming."

"I'm Joanne Kilbourn," I said. "I knew your brother many years ago in Toronto and I was a friend of Sally Love's."

She flinched but she looked at me steadily. "I was a friend of Sally's, too. I didn't see her often enough, but I loved to be with her. She always made me laugh. She made Izaak laugh, too. He used to say she'd lead him to an early grave, but he worshipped her."

Now it was my turn to flinch, but I reached out and touched her hand. "I know he worshipped her," I said. I grasped for something else to say. "Miss Levin, I'm truly sorry his life ended so unhappily."

She covered my hand with her own. "So, do you think he did what they said?"

The question took me by surprise, and so did my answer.

"No," I said, "I don't. They have all that evidence against him, but I just don't believe it."

"You don't believe it because it's not true," she said flatly. "He was my brother for sixty-five years. I knew his limits. He was no killer. He was a gambler, and like a lot of smart people he wasn't smart about money. You would have been a fool to cosign a loan with him, but killing? Never. Izaak Levin was no killer."

I didn't know what to say, so I said nothing. In the background, I could hear the sounds of the musicians packing up: instrument cases shutting, plans being made for lunch. I wondered if they knew how lucky they were to be part of the normal world.

For a moment Ellie Levin seemed to be lost in her thoughts. Finally she said, "He was in a lot of trouble when he died."

"Money trouble?" I asked.

"Worse," she said. "In-over-your-head trouble. It started with money. Before Christmas it was money. He called me Christmas Eve and told me he was seriously in need of cash."

"Did you give it to him?"

"Do I look crazy? I'm not a wealthy woman, Joanne. All I have is my home and some bonds our parents left me. I've always been firm with Izaak about money. I had to be. I was saving for our old age. I always figured somehow we'd end up together at the end of our lives, and I wanted things to be nice."

For a moment, I thought she was going to break, but she took a deep breath and went on.

"I talked to him two more times before . . . before the end. It was after New Year's Day, but I don't remember the days. Who remembers days when it's just ordinary life going on? Anyway, the first time, Izaak was on top of the world. 'No more money worries. I'll be your banker from now on, Ellie.' That's what he said. Of course, I tried to get him to tell me the particulars, but he just laughed.

"He wasn't laughing the last time he called. He sounded screwed up tight and frightened. This time when he wouldn't tell me what was going on, I didn't take no for an answer. I kept at him. I badgered him until finally he hung up on me. But I didn't give up even then. I phoned him back. He sounded so tired it broke my heart, but I was scared, too. I pleaded with him. I told him I'd keep calling him until he confided in me. Finally, he said, 'You always were persistent. But you know, sometimes it's safer not to know. I found out something I wasn't supposed to know, and now I'm out past Jackson's Point, Ellie. I'm way past Jackson's Point.'" She looked at me, waiting.

"I'm sorry," I said. "I don't understand."

"It was a place we weren't supposed to swim past when we were kids. Every summer there were stories about kids who swam past Jackson's Point and got caught in the weeds and were never seen again. Anyway, for Izaak and me, Jackson's Point became a way of saying we were in over our heads." Suddenly her eyes were filled with tears. "So I should have listened, right? Miss Practical saving for the future while the weeds are pulling my brother under."

"Have you told the police this?"

"Oh, yes," she said, "they were very patient. They heard me out and they asked me if I thought Izaak was involved in blackmail. When I said that's exactly what I was afraid of, they pounced. All the more proof of his guilt, they said. If Izaak knew he was going to be exposed, he might have killed Sally so she'd never know what he'd done." She looked directly at me, and there was a flash in her eyes that was very like her brother's. When she spoke again, her tone was like his, too: sardonic, mocking. "So," she said, "does that make sense to you? To kill someone you love so they won't think less of you?"

Her question was still in my ears as I walked across the snowy lawn in front of the fine arts building. There were other questions, too. If there was blackmail, who had been the target? Stuart Lachlan? If Stuart was the one, what was he being blackmailed about? How was Clea Poole involved? She and Izaak had little use for one another. Sally had told me that, but they both loved Sally. Had they discovered something condemning about Stuart Lachlan and decided . . . Decided what? And the one question that suddenly loomed over everything. If Izaak hadn't committed the murders who had? Who had killed Sally Love?

As I turned onto the street where I'd parked, my head was pounding. I was tired. I couldn't seem to work out any of the permutations and combinations, and I didn't want to. I wanted to go home and stand under the shower until all the horrors were washed away.

But the horrors were just beginning.

There was a traffic ticket on the window of the Mercedes. Except when I got closer I saw that it wasn't a traffic ticket.

It was an envelope, square, creamy, good quality. I opened it. Inside on a square of matching paper a message was printed in careful block letters: I SAW YOU KILL SALLY LOVE.

My first thought was that the note was some kind of bizarre sendoff for Izaak. But Izaak was dead. Twenty minutes earlier, the small mahogany box that held his earthly remains had been sitting on a table in the fine arts building. He was beyond messages. And the envelope hadn't been delivered to the funeral. It had been stuck on the windshield of my car.

Except it wasn't my car. The silvery Mercedes with the characteristic ARTS licence plate didn't belong to me. It belonged to Stuart Lachlan. The accusation of murder hadn't been directed at me; it was directed at Stuart Lachlan. I got into the car. My hands were shaking so badly I had trouble getting the key in the ignition.

I started to drive to Spadina Crescent. Then I thought about the nature of my evidence: an anonymous letter, a sister's belief that someone other than her brother was a killer. Why was I so ready to believe Stuart Lachlan was capable of murder? We had never been close, but I had liked him well enough. I'd been a guest in his home. I was his dead wife's oldest friend.

Things had gone very wrong for Stuart in the past months. There was no denying that, but Stu was a civilized man, and civilized people don't commit murder when things go wrong. As I turned onto my street, I thanked my lucky stars that I hadn't jeopardized my relationship with Stu and Taylor by levelling hysterical accusations at him. I'd always considered my two best qualities loyalty and common sense and I didn't seem to be exhibiting either. What I needed was rest and a chance to put things like an anonymous accusation into perspective.

Angus was running out the front door when I got home. "I left you a note. James asked me to sleep over. His parents are taking us to the Globetrotters and his mom says it'll be late so if it's okay with you I'll stay there. I know it's a school night, but I thought maybe for the Globetrotters, you could bend your rules."

I was glad to see him excited about something again. "For the Globetrotters, I'll bend," I said. "Have you got money?"

"Their treat," he said happily. "Thanks, Mum. I'll get my stuff after school."

"If I don't connect with you then, have a good time."

"Right," he said as he kissed the air near my face and ran out the door. He was back in a second.

"You'll be all right alone, won't you?" he asked.

"Absolutely," I said.

"It's all over, isn't it?" he said.

"Yeah," I said, "it's all over."

"It's all over," I repeated, as I stepped under the shower. But in my bones I knew that it wasn't over, and I was filled with apprehension.

It was when I was zipping my blue jeans that I remembered the package Sally Love had left at my house the night we came back from skiing at Greenwater. "My insurance policy," she'd called it. "If you lose it, I'm dead. And don't get curious."

Well, I hadn't lost it, but suddenly I was curious. The myth of Pandora's box didn't scare me. I couldn't imagine loosing any more evils on mankind than the horrors we'd already seen. I pulled on the sweater Nina had given me for Christmas. The pattern was an elaborate and brilliant patchwork of colours. Nina said it had taken her most of the month of November to finish it. Just putting it on made me feel close to her.

The package wrapped in brown paper was right where I had left it, in my sewing basket. I tore the wrapping off and found a videotape.

"Surprises," I said as I walked down the hall to our family room. *Young Frankenstein* was in the VCR. Angus and I had watched it together the night before. I pushed eject, then I put in Sally's tape, sat back in the rocking chair and watched.

For the first seconds I thought that somehow I'd erased the tape. The screen was filled with grey static, but then I saw a long shot of Stuart Lachlan's house. There was no sound, and the quality of the video wasn't very good. There was a close-up of Taylor's family of snow people, the father, the mother and the little snow girl with her sign – "Merry Christmas from Taylor." Home movies. The camera lingered a little on the snow people and then it moved down the flagstone walk past the stand of pine trees at the corner of the house and around to the backyard. Somehow the movement seemed purposeful, as if the person behind the camera had a plan in mind. There was a quick establishing shot of the backyard and then we were looking through a window. I recognized the room immediately. There was a wall of books and family pictures, a cabinet filled with Royal Doulton figurines and, over the mantel of the fireplace, a portrait of Sally and Taylor. The room was Stuart Lachlan's study at the back of the house.

There were people in the shot, and at first I couldn't make any sense of what they were doing. The quality of the film wasn't good – grey and grainy and unfocused. But then the focus was adjusted and I saw. There were two figures, a man and a woman. Both were naked. The man was on the floor on all fours in a position of submission. Behind him the woman raised what looked like a pony whip and brought it down on his back. He flinched but he didn't move. She raised the whip again. And again and again. Finally the whipping stopped. He rolled over and she lowered herself onto his erect penis.

I didn't watch any more. I didn't have to. I'd seen enough. The man on the floor was Stuart Lachlan, and the woman

who first beat him and then guided him into her body
was Nina Love. My heart was pounding, and the blood was
singing in my ears, but I didn't hesitate. I knew what I had to
do. I pushed the eject button and threw the tape into my bag.
I went upstairs, put on my ski jacket and boots, got into the
Mercedes and drove to Stuart Lachlan's house.

# CHAPTER

# 13

By the time I turned off the University Bridge the place behind the scar on my forehead was aching so badly I thought I was going to have to pull over. I could hear my mother's voice: "Nina may have fooled you, Joanne, but she never fooled me. She never fooled me."

"Shut up," I said, "just shut up. Let me work this out." The tape was terrible, but I couldn't let my horror over the video of Nina blind me to the significance of the tape itself. I had no doubt about the identity of the person who had held the camera. After all, I'd been in her sights myself New Year's Eve. Clea Poole had been everywhere with her video camera during those last days of the old year – "Mouse and her faithful Brownie," Sally had called her.

The tape was the missing piece in so many puzzles. Its existence explained Stu's sudden change of heart about Taylor's custody. ("Sally, did you sell your soul to the devil?" I had asked, and she had laughed. "No, to a mouse.") The tape was the explanation for the envelope of money Nina had taken to Izaak Levin's – not as an advance on a favourable book review, as Stuart Lachlan had told Nina, but

to keep a humiliating image of himself buried. He had succeeded; Stu's sexual practices were not a matter of public
record. But increasingly it looked as if a worse image of him
was about to emerge: the image of a man who had cold-
bloodedly murdered three people because they stood in the
way of how he believed his life should be lived.

I had no plan when I rang the doorbell of the Lachlan
house on Spadina Crescent. Somehow I had to warn Nina so
we could get Taylor out before . . . Before what? I didn't
know. My mind was numb. I couldn't seem to think beyond
the next moment. No one came to the door.

"Please, please, please," I said, as I rang the bell again, but
there was only silence and the sound of the blood singing in
my ears. I followed Clea Poole's route to the backyard: down
by the stone wall, past the stand of pine trees, along the
snowy flagstone walk.

I banged at the back door. I think I knew there'd be no
answer. I pulled the keys to the Mercedes out of my bag.
They were on a chain with other keys. I tried one that
looked like a house key, and first time lucky, the kitchen
door opened and I was inside.

On the round oak table by the window were the remains
of breakfast: three juice glasses, a half-empty milk glass,
three porridge bowls. I wondered if Goldilocks had felt as
scared as I did. I called Nina's name, then Taylor's. Finally,
tentatively, hoping there would be no answer, I called for
Stuart. There was nothing but silence. As I moved through
the house, I felt a coldness in the pit of my stomach. The
living and dining rooms were immaculate, but in the bed-
rooms the beds were unmade, and drawers and cupboard
doors gaped. It looked as if they had left in a hurry.

I left Stuart's study till the last. I don't know what I was
afraid of – a scarlet letter marking the place on the rug where
Stu and Nina had performed their strange act of love? I had

to steel myself to open the door, but there was nothing there. An innocent room filled with books and family pictures, a display case where Stuart's mother's collection of Royal Doulton ladies smiled and poured tea and bowed to one another, and over the mantel the portrait of Sally and Taylor, mother and daughter.

On the desk there was a telephone with an answering machine. I pressed the button to hear the message they had recorded for callers. No clues to where they had gone there; it was the same message I'd heard a dozen times over the winter. "This is Stuart Lachlan. Nina and Taylor and I are unable to come to the phone right now, but if you'll leave your name . . ."

I pushed the button again. "This is Stuart Lachlan. Nina and Taylor and I . . ." I pulled open Stuart's desk drawer. Shoved inside, not hidden, was a square envelope, the twin of the one I'd found on the Mercedes. I opened it. There was a note: THE CAMERA SAW WHAT YOU DID. There was also part of a photographer's contact sheet with eight proofs of pictures on it. I recognized them immediately as the ones the woman Anya had taken the night of the dinner. THE CAMERA SAW WHAT YOU DID. The camera saw, but I couldn't. The proof of Stuart's guilt was in my hand, but I couldn't see it. The pictures were so small I couldn't make out anything beyond the identity of the people at the table. Sally was in all of them: sitting between Stu and Izaak and looking miserable; leaning across Stu to say something to me; looking up at the camera as Nina stood behind her; scowling at Izaak as Stu leaned across her plate. I looked at that last picture again. It had to be the one. I couldn't make out what Stu was doing, but I thought I could see his hand close to Sally's plate.

"You're a killer, Stu." I tried the words aloud. They sounded right. "Well, you're not going to win this time, Stuart. I'm going to find you, and I'm going to make sure you

pay." I picked up the phone book and found the number of
the city police. On the other end of the line, the man's voice
told me Inspector Mary Ross McCourt was unavailable,
could he help. I thought of what would happen next. The
search for Stuart and Nina. The media announcements.
Nina's private life suddenly becoming public knowledge. I
imagined Nina somewhere answering the door, and strange
men in uniforms surrounding her, questioning her. What
Stuart had done was not her fault. She loved him. I remembered the videotape. The thought of strangers sitting in a
dimly lit room in police headquarters watching Nina's
nakedness made my stomach turn.

"Can anyone else help you?" the voice on the other end
of the line asked.

"No," I said, "no one can help me," and I hung up. There
was a personal telephone directory on the desk. How did you
list your own summer house? I was halfway through the
alphabet when I thought about S for Stay Away Lake.

The phone rang a dozen times before it was picked up.
The voice on the other end was Nina's. It seemed like a good
omen. I hadn't thought where to begin, but I knew I had to
keep her from reacting in case she wasn't alone.

"Nina, it's Jo. Is Stuart there with you?"

"No, he's out taking Taylor for a walk down by the lake,
but I can get him. Joanne, is something wrong?"

"Yes, Ni, something's wrong. Something's terribly wrong.
You have to get Taylor and come back to the city right away."

"Is there a problem with your family?"

"No, my family's fine. Ni, please get back here."

"Joanne, we just got unpacked. Stuart's exhausted. I can't
ask him to turn around and drive back to the city. He needs
time to heal."

"Fuck Stuart," I said. "Nina, you and Taylor have to get
out of there. I know I'm not making sense. Too much has

happened. It looks like Izaak Levin isn't the murderer after all. Ni, prepare yourself for some terrible news. I think Stuart is deeply implicated in the murders. You have to get out of there."

The silence on the other end of the line lasted so long I was afraid that Stuart had come into the room. But finally Nina answered me.

"Joanne, come and get me. Come and get us both. If Stuart has done what you say he did, I'm afraid of what will happen if I try to leave. Please, Jo. I've never asked much of you, but I'm asking this. Please, please come and get us."

The area behind my scar was throbbing. A steady beat of pain. I closed my eyes, and the image of Nina was there, lovely, loving, caring about me when no one else did. The one constant in my life.

"Of course," I said, "Ni, just hold on. I'll be right there."

"Do you know the way?"

"I can find it."

"If you start now, you'll be here before dark. Taylor and I will be at the dock waiting for you. Don't worry about driving across the lake. I know it's been warm, but the man at the crossing says the ice is safe. We'll be waiting."

It was a three-hour drive from the city to the Lachlan cottage on the island at Stay Away Lake. Three hours to think about the unthinkable. Sally's death was the perfect solution for Stu: no more problems about custody; no more threats to blow him out of the water over the stupid book he'd written. With Sally dead, Stu had it all. But he wasn't going to get it. When I saw the turnoff sign, I was filled with relief. It was almost over.

I looked at the lake. The ice was the colour of pewter, but there were dark places, too. There are often wonderful legends about these northern lakes, but the story of how Stay Away Lake got its name was not appealing. Local people said

that at the turn of the century a madman lived on the island
where the Lachlans later built their cottage. He killed anyone
who came near the island and he dumped their bodies in the
water – a dozen in all, they said, before finally he turned his
rifle on himself. The legend was that at night you could hear
the voices of his victims calling up their warning from the
lake bottom: "Stay away. Stay away. Stay away."

The old man at the landing was not as sanguine about the
ice as Nina had been. "It's been warm and the ice is punky,"
he said. "If I was you, I'd leave my car doors open, in case I
had to make a quick getaway out there."

So I drove with the doors of the Mercedes open, and
thought about the lost souls a few feet beneath me in the
weedy darkness, crying out their warnings.

Finally, I made out the point where the Lachlans had built
their cottage and I saw Nina and Taylor, two small figures
in bright ski clothes standing on the dock in front of the
boathouse.

I stopped the car at the far end of the dock. I didn't like the
look of the ice closer to shore. Taylor ran out to meet me.

"Your car doors are open," she said. "We watched you drive
across, and your doors were open all the way. Did you forget?"

"It's just the way you drive on ice," I said, "to be safe."

"You wouldn't want to go through," she said sagely. "You'd
hurt all the fish down on the bottom waiting for spring."

"I was careful," I said. "No one got hurt. I promise."

Nina hadn't moved. She was still standing in front of the
boathouse. Taylor and I walked to her. I didn't like the way
Nina looked; she was composed but very pale. Her ski jacket
was a brilliant blue. When she'd bought it, she'd asked me if
the style was too young for her. That day, as she'd stood in
the Ski Shoppe slender and glowing with happiness, I'd said,
"Nothing will ever be too young for you." I couldn't have
said that now.

"Are you ready?" I asked her.

Her eyes widened. It seemed as if she had just noticed I was there.

"No," she said in a low, flat voice, "I'm not ready."

"Nina, we have to go."

She raised her hand as if she were warding something off. "I have to look at him. I have to tell him that I know what he did. I have to finish it."

She turned and went into the boathouse. I followed her. It was dark in there and cold. The air smelled of fish and dampness, but intermingled with the lake smells was the scent of Nina's perfume. When she opened the door on the other side, a shaft of pale light came toward me, but she was in darkness.

"Ni, I'm coming with you," I said.

When she answered, her voice was terrible.

"No, Jo. This is private. Just for me alone. Please, go and stay with Taylor. She'll be frightened. I'll be back. I can't just walk away from him." She stepped outside and pulled the door shut after her.

I walked through the boathouse. Taylor was waiting at the end of the dock. She had the mass card from Sally's funeral in her hand. I'd left it on the dash of the Mercedes. I came and looked over her shoulder at the picture on the front: Sally's present to me. "Hang on to it, it's the only picture I ever did of Nina. She's so beautiful I could almost forgive her." Beside me, Taylor traced the perfect circle that enclosed Sally and Desmond Love.

"Did Nina put them there?" she asked.

"What?" I said stupidly.

Her voice was small and patient. "Did Nina put Sally and my grandfather under the water?"

I looked at the picture. Sally's golden head bent toward Desmond Love's – they had never needed anyone else.

Daughter and father, absorbed, happy, complete, as together they built sand castles in the perfect circle of their private world.

In that moment I knew.

"Get in the car, and no matter what happens, stay there. I'll be back for you. I promise. Just stay there."

I ran through the boathouse. The scent of Joy lingered like a memory. I was halfway up the hill when I heard the first shot. It sounded dry and inconsequential, and then I heard the second.

At the top of the hill, the lights from the cottage shone yellow and welcoming in the dusk. A place to come home to.

When I got to the door I was overwhelmed with a sense of déjà vu so violent it was physical. Another cottage. Another night. Thirty-two years before. And I had stood there looking past Izaak Levin into the cottage, and I had seen . . .

I had seen exactly what Nina Love had planned that I would see. Hilda McCourt had quoted Graham Greene: "There is always one moment in childhood when the door opens and lets the future in."

That had been my moment. If I hadn't gone back to my cottage for my shoes, I would have been the one who walked in and found them. But it was Izaak who found them. I was late. She had taken a risk with that poison. My father said that another half hour would have tipped the balance. But, of course, I would never have made Nina wait another half hour. She knew I would come. She knew she could count on me to make her plan work. And it had worked. Des was dead. Sally had been so shattered she was easily disposed of, and Nina was rich and free of an invalid husband and a daughter who would always be her rival. She had taken a risk, but she knew the risk was minimal because she had me.

And now she had taken another risk. I knew she was behind that door waiting, waiting for me to come in, so the performance could begin. She knew she could count on me. Whatever story she told me, I would believe. I would swear to.

I almost walked away, but then I thought of Sally and Des and Izaak and Clea and the Righteous Protester – debts waiting to be discharged. I reached out and turned the doorknob.

Stu was lying face down on the floor. Nina spun around when she heard me. The gun was still in her hand.

"Oh, thank God, Jo, it was terrible, he pulled the gun. You were right, it was Stuart all along."

I was crying. I couldn't recognize my voice. "No, Nina, not Stuart. It wasn't Stuart. And it wasn't Izaak and it wasn't Des. It was you, Nina. It was you. I loved you, and it was you. All these years. It was you."

I looked at her and I saw that imperceptibly she had raised the gun. It was pointed at me now.

"It had to be done, Jo." She shook her head in a gesture of impatience I'd seen a thousand times. "Jo, I had to . . . Sometimes people have to act. Otherwise lives would just go off course." She moved closer. The gun was still pointed at me. "I wish you hadn't stopped being loyal, Jo." She raised the gun.

In that pleasant cottagey room, there was the scent of Joy, and other smells, not flowery, not pleasant: the smells of death and of fear. The smell of death was Stuart's, but the fear was mine.

Suddenly, behind me, there was a small voice. Clear and clearly frightened.

"Are you going to kill us all, Nina?" Taylor asked.

Nina shifted her gaze for a moment, and I moved toward her and smashed at her hand. She looked quickly at me, astounded, as if the ground had suddenly opened beneath her feet.

The gun was still in her hand, but it was pointed toward the floor now. Nina couldn't seem to take her eyes from Taylor's face. She began backing away from her granddaughter, past Stuart into the living room. Finally, when her back was against the big plate-glass window that looked out on the woods, she stopped. On the other side of the window the aspens shivered in the pink-gold light of the dropping sun.

There were no last words. Nina looked quickly at me, then at Taylor. Then she turned to face the aspens and raised the gun to her temple – the barrel touched her temple at just the point where the dark curve of her hair hit the flawless plane of her cheek. Yin and yang.

I didn't go to her. I turned and put my arm around Taylor's shoulder, and after forty-seven years I walked out on Nina Love. By the time Taylor and I got to the dock, the sun was low, and the ice glowed with the cool colours of a northern winter: white, purple, blue, grey. But across the lake, in the west, the sky was the most incredible shade of pink.

I pointed to it as we got into the car. "Your favourite colour," I said.

"Not any more," she said.

In that moment, there was an inflection in Taylor's voice that sounded just like her mother's. We looked at each other and then, without another word, we drove across the fragile ice to the safety of the shore.

# CHAPTER

# 14

Taylor is with us now. She came home with me that night and she never left. There was, in fact, nowhere else for her to go. Stuart and Sally were both only children. Stu had an old aunt in a nursing home somewhere in Ontario, but Sally had no one. Nina had seen to that.

The morning after she came, Taylor and I walked over to the campus together. It was a pretty day, and we bought hot chocolate from a machine and took it outside so we could watch the squirrels. I told her that our family wanted her to live with us, and we wondered how she felt. For a while she didn't say anything. Then she looked at me.

"Is it taken care of?" she asked.

"It can be," I said.

"Good," she said and that was the end of it. She hasn't brought up the subject since. My old friend Ali Sutherland, who's a psychiatrist, flew in from Winnipeg to talk to her. She said Taylor is doing as well as any child could after what Ali called "an appalling and crushing series of traumas." Indeed. What Taylor needs, says Ali, is counselling, reassurance and routine – constant reinforcement of the knowledge that everything in her new home is fixed and permanent. "Forever," Ali had added for emphasis.

And so we do our best. So far, our best seems to be good enough. Taylor is beginning to trust us. The rest will, I hope, come later.

The final murder investigation was swift and decisive, and that helped. I didn't have to produce the tape of Stuart and Nina, and that helped, too. The day after I got back from Stay Away Lake, the police discovered a tape that made mine irrelevant. This tape had been in the video camera above the bridal bed at the gallery, and it showed Nina killing Clea Poole. "Murder as performance art," Hugh Rankin-Carter said when he called to see how I was taking this latest blow. I was glad they found the tape. I didn't want there to be any doubts.

Now there weren't.

This final unassailable proof of Nina's guilt was discovered under circumstances that make me believe in cosmic justice or at least in cosmic jokes. When the police searched Izaak Levin's house, they found a key stuck to the back of the self-portrait Sally had painted for Izaak when she was fourteen. The key was to a safety-deposit box Izaak had rented under the name Desmond Love. The tape was there, and with it was a long and incoherent letter addressed to Sally. When the police sorted through all the justifications and mea culpas, the history of the tape and the role it played in Sally's death became clear.

The night Clea Poole was murdered, Izaak Levin went to the gallery to check on the installation Clea was working on. The young woman who had created the piece was a talented conceptual artist whom Izaak was thinking of taking on as a client. He had told several people at the gallery that the installation had to be executed perfectly and that he was concerned that Clea Poole was too sick to do the job right.

When he arrived, Clea was dead and the video camera was whirring away above the bed. Sally had made no secret about the disintegration of her relationship with Clea, and Izaak had assumed Sally was the murderer. To protect the woman he had loved for thirty years, he ripped the tape out and took it home for safekeeping. If he hadn't given in to his curiosity, Sally might have lived. But when Izaak looked at the tape, two things came together for him: his own financial need and the knowledge that he had hard proof Nina Love was guilty of murder. The blackmail began, and the chain of circumstances that ended in Sally's death and his own was set in motion.

Izaak had to die. He threatened not only Nina's freedom but also the family life she had so carefully crafted after she came to Saskatoon. As long as he lived, Nina's happiness hung by a thread. But Izaak Levin wasn't the only threat.

Nina had always seen Sally as her rival: first with Desmond Love, then with Stuart Lachlan and Taylor. As Sally's plans for taking her daughter with her to Vancouver took shape, Nina's plan to kill Sally took shape. It was Anya the photographer who showed how the murder was done. When the proofs on the contact sheet were enlarged, the police saw what Anya had seen: Sally's evening bag slung over the back of her chair seconds before Nina passed by but missing after she left. After Nina went to the cloakroom and slipped Sally's bag with the epinephrine into the pocket of Izaak Levin's coat, she came back to the table and put the powdered almonds on Sally's dessert. Izaak was so drunk it would have been easy for her to slip the empty bag into his pocket.

Nina never had to put the next part of her plan into effect. She never had to kill Izaak Levin. He died all on his own. It was the one lucky break she had. But Nina Love had never relied on luck. When the police opened the locked door of her room in the Lachlan house, they found enough prescription drugs to kill ten men. All the drugs were perfectly legal, the kind of medications a charming woman with a flair for acting could get a doctor to prescribe for her. The kind of drugs that could easily and fatally be slipped into a shot of whisky and offered to a drunk in a state of shock.

We'll never know, but as Mary Ross McCourt said, the one thing we know for certain is that Nina Love would not have allowed Izaak Levin to leave the Mendel Gallery alive that night. And so it's over.

Hilda McCourt came by today with a brochure for Shakespeare on the Saskatchewan. This summer they'll be doing *Twelfth Night*, and Hilda wants to take the kids. When she was leaving she looked into the living room. Angus was putting the finishing touches on a diorama for his biology project, and Taylor was drawing the morpheus butterfly that's going to be the star of the show.

For a moment, Hilda watched them without comment, then she touched my arm.

"I used to tell my students that at the end of a satisfying piece of fiction there is always something lost but there's also something gained. Try not to lose sight of that, Joanne."

I watched as Hilda got into her old Austin Healey and drove off. What I have lost still overwhelms me: Izaak, Stuart, Sally, Nina. Me. Or at least that part of me that believed the magic of life could be found in Nina and her world of eyelet dresses and dappled sunlight on the tea table and mist hanging heavy on the lake. All of this is gone, and much of it is, I know, past recovery.

But as I stand here on this, the first day of spring, watching my new daughter transform the blank page of an ordinary school notebook into the electric-blue flash of an Amazon butterfly, I repeat Hilda's words like a mantra. Something was lost, but something was gained. Something was lost but something was gained.

If you enjoyed

# MURDER AT THE MENDEL

treat yourself to all of the
Joanne Kilbourn mysteries,
now available in stunning new
trade paperback editions
and as eBooks

McCLELLAND & STEWART

*www.mcclelland.com*

*www.mysterybooks.ca*

# DEADLY APPEARANCES

When Andy Boychuk drops dead at a political picnic, the evidence points to his wife. Joanne takes her first "case" as Canada's favourite amateur sleuth as she seeks to clear Eve Boychuk, discovering along the way a Bible college that isn't all it seems . . .

**"A compelling novel infused with a subtext that's both inventive and diabolical."** – Montreal *Gazette*

Trade Paperback 978-0-7710-1324-9          Ebook 978-0-7710-1322-5

---

# MURDER AT THE MENDEL

Joanne's childhood friend, Sally Love, is an artist who courts controversy. When Sally's former partner turns up dead, Joanne discovers the past they shared was much more complicated, sordid, and deadly than she ever guessed.

**"Classic. . . . enough twists to qualify as a page turner. . . . Bowen and her genteel sleuth are here to stay."** – Saskatoon *StarPhoenix*

Trade Paperback 978-0-7710-1321-8          Ebook 978-0-7710-1320-1

---

# THE WANDERING SOUL MURDERS

Joanne's peace is destroyed when her daughter finds a young woman's body near her shop. The next day, her son's girlfriend drowns, an apparent suicide. When it is discovered that the two young women had at least one thing in common, Joanne is drawn into a twilight world where money can buy anything.

**"With her rare talent for plumbing emotional pain, Bowen makes you feel the shock of murder."** – *Kirkus Reviews*

Trade Paperback 978-0-7710-1319-5          Ebook 978-0-7710-1318-8

## A COLDER KIND OF DEATH

When the man convicted of murdering her husband six years earlier is himself shot, Joanne is forced to relive the most horrible time of her life. But it soon gets much worse when the prisoner's menacing wife is found dead a few nights later, strangled with Joanne's own silk scarf . . .

**"A terrific story with a slick twist at the end."**
– *Globe and Mail*

Trade Paperback 978-0-7710-1317-1          Ebook 978-0-7710-1316-4

## A KILLING SPRING

The head of the School of Journalism at Joanne's university is found in a seedy rooming house wearing only women's lingerie and an electrical cord around his neck. When other events indicate that it was not a case of accidental suicide, Joanne finds herself deep in a world of fear, deceit, and danger.

**"A compelling novel as well as a gripping mystery."**
– *Publishers Weekly*

Trade Paperback 978-0-7710-1315-7          Ebook 978-1-5519-9613-4

## VERDICT IN BLOOD

The corpse of the respected — and feared — Judge Justine Blackwell is found in a Regina park. Joanne tries to help a good friend involved in a struggle over which of Blackwell's wills is valid, and those who stand to lose the inheritance may well be murderers willing to strike again.

**"An entirely satisfying example of why Gail Bowen has become one of the best mystery writers in the country."**
– *London Free Press*

Trade Paperback 978-0-7710-1311-9          Ebook 978-1-5519-9614-1

# BURYING ARIEL

Ariel Warren, a young colleague at Joanne's university, is stabbed to death in the library, and two men are under suspicion. The apparently tight-knit academic community is bitterly divided, vengeance is in the air, and Joanne is desperate to keep the wrong person from being punished for Ariel's death.

"Nearly flawless plotting, characterization, and writing." – *London Free Press*

Trade Paperback 978-0-7710-1309-6          Ebook 978-1-5519-9615-8

# THE GLASS COFFIN

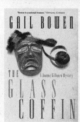

Joanne's friend Jill is about to marry a celebrated documentary filmmaker, both of whose previous wives committed suicide – after he had made films about them. When the best man's dead body is found just hours before the ceremony, Joanne begins to truly fear for her friend's safety.

"Chilling and unexpected." – *Globe and Mail*

Trade Paperback 978-0-7710-1305-8          Ebook 978-1-5519-9616-5

# THE LAST GOOD DAY

Joanne is on holiday at a cottage in an exclusive enclave owned by lawyers from the same prestigious firm. When one of them kills himself the night after a long talk with Joanne, she is pushed into an investigation that has startling – and possibly fatal – consequences.

"A classic whodunit in which everything from setting to plot to character works beautifully.... A treat from first page to final paragraph." – *Globe and Mail*

Trade Paperback 978-0-7710-1349-2          Ebook 978-1-5519-9617-2

# THE ENDLESS KNOT

After journalist Kathryn Morrissey publishes a tell-all book on the adult children of Canadian celebrities, one of the parents angrily confronts her and as a result is charged with attempted murder. When the parent hires Zack Shreve, the new love in Joanne's life, to defend him, her own understanding of the knot that binds parent and child becomes both personal and very urgent.

"A late-night page turner. . . . A rich and satisfying read." – *Edmonton Journal*

Trade Paperback 978-0-7710-1347-8          Ebook 978-1-5519-9246-4

# THE BRUTAL HEART

A local call girl is dead, and her impressive client list includes the name of Joanne's new husband. Shaken that Zack saw the woman regularly before they met, Joanne throws herself into her work and is soon embroiled in a bitter and increasingly strange custody battle of a local MP, who is simultaneously trying to win an election.

"Elegant. . . . Joanne rules the narrative. [*The Brutal Heart*] slips along with grace and style." – *Toronto Star*

Trade Paperback 978-0-7710-0994-5          Ebook 978-1-5519-9233-4

# THE NESTING DOLLS

Just before she is murdered, a young woman hands her baby to a perfect stranger and disappears. The stranger is the daughter of lawyer Delia Wainberg, and soon a secret from Delia's youth comes out. Not only is a killer on the loose, but the dead woman's partner is demanding custody of the child, and the battle threatens to tear apart Joanne's own family.

"The underlying human drama of love and good intentions gone very, very bad make the novel a compelling read." – *Vancouver Sun*

Trade Paperback 978-0-7710-1276-1          Ebook 978-0-7710-1277-8

*Edward Willet*

GAIL BOWEN's first Joanne Kilbourn mystery, *Deadly Appearances* (1990), was nominated for the W.H. Smith/ Books in Canada Best First Novel Award. It was followed by *Murder at the Mendel* (1991), *The Wandering Soul Murders* (1992), *A Colder Kind of Death* (1994) (which won an Arthur Ellis Award for best crime novel), *A Killing Spring* (1996), *Verdict in Blood* (1998), *Burying Ariel* (2000), *The Glass Coffin* (2002), *The Last Good Day* (2004), *The Endless Knot* (2006), *The Brutal Heart* (2008), and *The Nesting Dolls* (2010). In 2008 *Reader's Digest* named Bowen Canada's Best Mystery Novelist; in 2009 she received the Derrick Murdoch Award from the Crime Writers of Canada. Bowen has also written plays that have been produced across Canada and on CBC Radio. Now retired from teaching at First Nations University of Canada, Gail Bowen lives in Regina. Please visit the author at www.gailbowen.com.